THE ACCIDENTAL ADVENTURERS
THE MYSTERY OF THE EMPTY HOUSE

THE ACCIDENTAL ADVENTURERS

THE MYSTERY OF THE EMPTY HOUSE

HENYE MEYER

Menucha Publishers, Inc.
© 2019 by Henye Meyer
Typeset and designed by Rivkah Lewis
All rights reserved

ISBN 978-1-61465-533-6
Library of Congress Control Number: 2019933441

Published and distributed by:
Menucha Publishers, Inc.
1235 38th Street
Brooklyn, NY 11218
Tel/Fax: 718-232-0856
www.menuchapublishers.com
sales@menuchapublishers.com

Printed in Israel

CONTENTS

CHAPTER 1

THE EMPTY HOUSE

Every time the three boys passed the big, vacant house, they stopped to stare at it. They always grouped themselves in the same way: Lemel in front, because he was the leader. On either side and slightly behind him, Fishel, the thin one, and Sender, the average one.

They had been together since they started school, partly because they lived near one another, partly because they were all in the same class, but especially because all three loathed their names, especially Fishel, who was an only child and whose mother sometimes called him "Fishy."

"Just imagine," Sender said, "if the postal service took it literally when people wrote 'Return to Sender' on letters they didn't want. Imagine how much junk mail I'd get!"

"Ha," Lemel grumbled. "At least for you, people have to know about writing things on letters. Everybody knows about sheep! And *lemelach*! I'm going to be the only sheep that stands up for itself! I even saw somewhere," he added, "that if a name is peculiar, people shouldn't give it. At least somebody out there had *rachmanus* on us."

There were two glum nods of approval. Still, most of the time the boys were able to ignore their names. They had been in cheder with the same classmates for so many years that eventually the boring old jokes about their names had mercifully lost their charm and been nearly forgotten.

Since they lived near one another, the three boys usually walked to cheder together. Their route took them past the old house, and they always peered into it.

Set well back from the road, up a driveway broken by weeds, the house was enormous — a mansion, really. A long, untended lawn ran from the sidewalk to the house, with ragged, overgrown shrubs facing the street. To one side of the driveway, at the back, stood a decaying garage, one door hanging crookedly.

The house was built of yellowish brick, with inset rows of ordinary red brick at every story. Above every window, and on each sill below, there was a carved stone decoration. It had been an expensive house, and a beautiful one, once.

All the ground-floor windows were boarded up to keep casual vandals out, but rows of dusty panes lined the upper stories. At the front and side of the lower two stories, curved bay windows swept outward gracefully.

The house was attached to another one next door, the mirror image of itself, but that one had long ago been sold and turned into a school. Some of Lemel's sisters had gone there.

The boys often walked around the outside of the house. There was nothing to tell them not to, and no gate across the driveway. There wasn't even a "For Sale" sign.

"Do you think there was a gate, once?" Fishel asked Lemel, who often could tell him what he wanted to know.

"There might have been," said Lemel, "a big, high one of wrought iron." He examined the stone gateposts. "Yes, here are the holes. Double gates."

"What happened to them?" Sender pressed forward to see the holes.

"I read that the government collected gates and railings to be melted down for guns, for the war," Lemel said. "They even collected pots."

"That was a long time ago," said Sender. "Why weren't the gates replaced?"

"After the war, a lot of rich people didn't have money any longer."

"Why not?" asked Fishel.

Lemel shrugged. "I didn't get that far."

Sender said, "Our house used to have a big wooden gate at the front of the garden. Maybe that's what people replaced the iron ones with."

"What happened to it?" Fishel asked.

"It rotted. It came off the hinges, and we had to throw it away."

Nobody asked why Sender's family hadn't replaced it. They didn't have money to spend on things that weren't absolutely necessary.

Fishel gazed up at the grand home. "It's a shame. I don't have anything against rich people being rich as long as they give some of it to poor people."

The others agreed with him. Together they walked on.

"You know," Fishel said suddenly, "it's Sukkos soon. We could build our own sukkah in the grounds of that house."

"Wouldn't it be trespassing?" Lemel asked. "Sometimes, even when there's no reason people won't let you use empty land. Grown-ups are funny."

"But we could do it in one of our own yards, couldn't we?" Sender suggested.

He knew it wouldn't be as much fun, but both his and Lemel's yards had space.

"You all know how tiny mine is," said Fishel. "Once our own sukkah is up, there's no room for anything else."

The others nodded.

"Well, I'm going to ask my father," Lemel decided.

"And I'll ask, too," said Sender. "But."

They all knew what that meant. Sender was near the top of his family. He was often sent on errands, or asked to babysit his little sisters and brother at home or in the yard while his mother took care of the housework.

"We'll have a hard time keeping my sisters out, though, if we do it in mine," Lemel warned them. He was the only boy, with a row of big sisters who were very loving but, he felt, far too interested in what he did. "If you can think of a way to chase them off…"

Fishel and Sender laughed. The only way they had ever found to keep Lemel's sisters away was by bringing Sender's little brother in. He bit. They could all picture themselves trying to stay away from Zevy's teeth in a tiny sukkah.

"I guess we'll just have to keep our eyes open for anybody visiting the mansion, then," said Lemel. "Maybe we should take turns going past more often, to have a better chance of catching somebody."

"Of course!" said Sender. "The owner or his property manager must go in to see that things are all right."

Fishel said, "I can probably get permission to go sometime after supper."

"We'll stick to business hours," decided Lemel. "But I think property managers do work Sundays."

"If we're doing something together, it won't matter if we go away for half an hour or so, will it?" said Fishel.

Turns were arranged, but the boys hadn't counted on preparations for yom tov. Their parents sent them on errands unpredictably, or gave them so many jobs that there was no time for them to gather. They hardly ever had a chance to even glance at the house, aside from the usual cheder route.

"This is crazy!" Fishel burst out as they walked past the house on the last day of classes. "At this rate, we'll never catch anybody!"

CHAPTER 2

WHAT'S INSIDE?

On a Sunday just before Sukkos, Lemel's mother and sisters were decorating their sukkah. Once, when business had been very good, Lemel's father had built a sukkah onto the house, so they no longer needed to worry about constructing one every year.

"We don't need you for this," said one of his sisters. "You can go play with your friends."

Lemel seized the opportunity to disappear, and ran to the old house.

Alone, he stood near the mouth of the overgrown driveway. Behind him, he heard the noise of a car. He turned and backed away to let it pass. The driver parked, walked into the broken-down garage facing the mansion on the other side of the driveway, and came out with a ring of keys dangling from his finger. A minute later, he was fitting one of the keys into a lock on the door.

Lemel ran up the driveway.

"Excuse me," he said breathlessly, "would you let me see inside this house, please?"

The man turned around. He saw a boy of about eleven or so dressed neatly in a sweater and pants. On the boy's face, glasses were sliding down his nose. He looked pretty harmless, the agent thought. Even respectable.

"I don't see why not," said the man, and, turning the key, he threw the door open. "As long as you stay near me. Some of the floors are bad."

"What about my two friends?"

The man paused. "Well, the house is pretty bare inside," he said at last. "Okay. But I'm only here for a few minutes today. There's only time to look at a couple of rooms."

"We'll have to get permission from our parents, first, anyway," Lemel said. "How often do you come?"

"Every two weeks. I can make it the Sunday after next, if you'd like. Around eleven thirty in the morning."

"Oh, boy, thank you!" Lemel said happily.

"And if you want to play outside, I'm sure the owner won't mind, as long as you don't do any damage."

"You really mean it?" Lemel could hardly catch his breath.

"Yeah, he's a nice guy. He'd love to fix up the old place, but he doesn't have the money. He says he likes kids, so he'd let you play on the grounds." He fished in a pocket. "Here's my card. Your mother will probably want to know where I work."

"Thanks!" Lemel pocketed the precious business card while the man gave the interior of the house a quick glance.

As Lemel followed the property manager back to his car, he asked, "I don't suppose it's haunted, is it?"

"Haunted! I hope not! Ghosts give me the creeps!" The property manager got into the car, waved, backed down to the street, and drove off.

Lemel could hardly wait to tell Fishel and Sender that they had permission to see inside the vast mansion. But when Lemel arrived at Fishel's house, he found his friend helping his father put up the sukkah. Fishel looked over his shoulder at Lemel.

"Don't talk to me," he warned him. "My father and I only have today to get the sukkah up. I don't think we'll even have time to decorate it this year."

Fishel's father traveled all week.

"It's all right," Lemel said, wanting Fishel to know he wasn't offended. "I won't bother you now. I'll tell you Chol HaMoed. It can wait."

He ran to his own house.

"Fishel's father is only just putting up their sukkah," Lemel said. "I don't think they have any decorations. Can we spare some?"

"What a good idea!" said Mommy. She picked out four big layered stars made of shiny paper. "How about these?" She added two posters in reasonably good condition. "We have more than we need, anyway."

Putting the decorations in a big carrier bag, Lemel brought them to Fishel. "I'm sorry to bother you," he said. "I'll go away soon, but can you use these? We have way too many for our sukkah. You can just use thumbtacks to put them up. I put some in the bag."

Fishel's face lit up. "All our old decorations got wet," he said. "Tatty, we have decorations after all!" he called up to his father, who was trying to bolt two walls together.

"Goog igea!" said his father. He was holding something with his mouth as well as with his hands.

Lemel laughed. Leaving them to their work, he went to see Sender. When Lemel arrived, Sender was just taking his little brother to the park.

"Why is it always you?" Lemel asked.

Sender groaned. "Mommy says Zevy is going through a difficult stage and I'm the only one who can handle him."

"Yeah?"

"I'm the only one he doesn't bite."

While Sender pushed Zevy on the swings, Lemel told him about meeting the property manager. "And he said he'll make sure to come around eleven thirty the Sunday morning after next so we can join him!" he finished.

"Hey, wow, it's still before cheder begins again! We can do it! I'd really like to see inside that place. Every time I walk past it I wonder what it's like. And while it's still Sukkos, we can build our own sukkah, too!" Sender's face fell. "I'll probably have to bring Zevy along, though. Even for the tour of the house. Do you think he'll mind?"

"Zevy or the property man?"

"The property manager!"

"What's the worst the man can do? Say no? You live practically around the corner. If you have to, you can leave Zevy at home for half an hour."

"Maybe. I'll make sure to find the harness, just in case. Honestly, sometimes I feel like I'm taking care of a pet dog. *L'havdil.*"

Lemel laughed. "Maybe you should teach him to bark!"

When the first day of Chol HaMoed came, Lemel ran down the street to Fishel's house, but Fishel and his parents were just piling into their old car.

"No time now!" Fishel called through the window. "My father's taking a day off for Chol HaMoed, and we're having a family outing!" He waved a jam jar at Lemel. It was in a mesh bag from oranges, and tied tightly with string. "Goldie says hello!"

Fishel had never been allowed a pet. His mother had a fur allergy. But when Fishel had won his goldfish at a fair, he had been allowed to keep it. He was so attached to it that he took it everywhere except cheder. He had named it Goldie, though he was convinced his goldfish was a boy fish, and always referred to it as "he."

While Fishel was out, Sender and Lemel started collecting things for the sukkah.

"We don't have much," Sender said. "We store our sukkah away every year. Every part is numbered. My father is very methodical. But there's this heap in the yard where he puts all the useful-looking stuff he doesn't want to throw out."

"I'll ask my mother for curtains, for the walls," said Lemel. "She's got boxes and boxes in the attic."

"You'll have to help me look through my father's pile," Sender said. "There's a big tarp over it, and it'll need both of us to pull it off."

The best find was a neat stack of cinder blocks. It would be a pain to move them, Lemel thought, but Sender's father did have a wheelbarrow, and the blocks would make a good base.

Fortunately, Sender's father was willing to let them have anything they wanted from his heap, as long as they brought it back again. And Lemel's mother gave him a huge armload of curtains, though she was plainly sorry to see them go.

CHAPTER 3

THE NEW SUKKAH

The next morning, Lemel rang Fishel's doorbell at nine thirty. Fishel's mother didn't look particularly happy when she came to the door. It looked as if Lemel had woken her up. But Fishel was fully dressed when he came bounding down the stairs, so Lemel figured she just hadn't been up for very long.

"Come tell me while I eat breakfast!" yelled Fishel. He was always eager and loud in the morning.

While Fishel worked his way through a bowl of cornflakes, a bowl of Rice Krispies, and a giant slice of leftover cake, Lemel told him about the house and about using the grounds.

"Did you hear that, Goldie?" Fishel asked his fish, now in its usual bowl on the table. Goldie ignored him. It usually did, except when Fishel dropped food in.

"I see why your father works so hard, Fishel," said Lemel. "You eat it all up!" He wondered where it all went. Fishel was skinny enough to slide through a mail slot.

Fishel just laughed. "About the sukkah," he said between bites, "we have lots of stuff! Poles to stick in the holes in the cinder blocks, and a few boards we can fasten to the tops of the poles, to hold the *schach*. We can build it something like the way the Mishkan was put together."

"You remember that?" Lemel asked, astonished. Fishel wasn't the best student in the class.

"We learn it every year. It has to sink in sometime," said Fishel, pleased that Lemel had noticed. "I know my father won't mind if we use some of his cable ties. We have about a million. And duct tape."

"We can't do without that," Lemel agreed. "My father says the universe is held together with duct tape!"

By noon, the boys had moved all the odds and ends to the old house's back garden. There was a good corner where the rear entrance and the house wall made a right angle. No tree branches reached that far.

"It's nice and level, too," said Fishel, beginning to lay out the first layer of cinder blocks in a neat rectangle.

Sender thought the best part was that it was completely hidden from the street. Vandals wouldn't notice it.

Although they used the cable ties, attaching the wood to the poles at the top wasn't simple. Fishel held up the big roll of duct tape. "I don't know if it's enough, but let's start it, anyway," he said.

In the end, both Lemel and Sender had to bring more duct tape from their homes. But it did work. At last, the frame at the top of the poles was sturdy enough to hold the support beams for the *schach*. There weren't many, though. Holding his breath, Lemel picked up an armload of old lulavim that he and Sender had found, and tossed them gently onto the narrow pieces of wood. The support beams held.

"Whew!" Lemel said. "I was afraid the whole thing would collapse."

It was Fishel's idea, too, to run a cord from the cable ties at each corner to hold the curtains. At the bottom, the curtains were fastened to the poles.

The boys stood looking proudly at their creation. It really was a fine sukkah!

As if the same thought had occurred to all of them at once, the three boys dived inside. They nearly knocked the whole sukkah down, but it held up — just — and they settled down on the ground.

Admittedly, the sukkah was not quite high enough for them to stand up in, but it didn't feel cramped, and its proportions were good.

The boys grinned at each other in triumphant silence.

"We can eat supper here tonight," Sender said.

"And breakfast tomorrow," said Lemel.

"I'll have to eat at home first," said Fishel. "I can't carry that much food at once. I'll just bring a snack along."

The other two laughed. Fishel's snacks were as big as meals!

That evening at supper, Lemel said, "The sukkah has come out really well."

"It's built in!" one of his sisters laughed.

"No, I mean ours, the one Fishel and Sender and I built," said Lemel.

"Where did you build it? In one of the yards?" his mother asked.

"No, in back of the big old deserted house," he said.

"What? But that's trespassing!" his sister objected.

"No, we got permission from the man who checks on the property," Lemel explained. He took an enormous forkful of chicken.

"When did you see him?" his mother asked.

Lemel chewed for a while until he could speak. "Just before yom tov. When he offered me the tour of the house," he said at last. "May I go, Mommy? He says the Sunday morning after Sukkos is good for him. Sender and Fishel want to come, too."

"What sort of person is this man?" his mother asked.

Lemel shrugged. "Just a man. He works for the property management company that takes care of the house."

"What was he wearing?"

Lemel tried to remember. "Uh, a jacket and pants. Nothing special. Oh — he gave me his business card." He dropped his fork and ran up to fetch the card from his room. "Here," he said, handing over the card and resuming his meal.

His mother looked at the card. "Oh, I know about this firm. They're very reputable," she said. "All right. It's fine with me."

The other boys, too, had permission to tour the house, they reported, although their parents had actually telephoned the property management agency to ask about the man. Every time they met at the sukkah, they looked around with pride. They had done a good job, and the continuing good weather meant they really did almost live in their very own sukkah.

CHAPTER 4

TOUR OF THE HOUSE

Once Sukkos was over and they had dismantled the whole structure and returned all the parts to their respective homes, they could think of nothing but the promised tour of the house. With every passing day, their excitement grew. Sunday felt as though it would never come.

"I've never been in a house that old," Fishel said for the fortieth time. "And Goldie will love a change of scenery!"

"Goldie probably won't notice," said Lemel crushingly. "I read somewhere that a goldfish's memory lasts only three seconds."

"That can't be true," Fishel objected. "Goldie knows to come up for food when I hold the box over his bowl, even before I put any in. He's really smart."

Finally, the appointed Sunday morning arrived. All

three boys were waiting at the old house well before eleven thirty, in plenty of time to see the property agent drive in.

When the agent got out of his car and saw that Sender was holding Zevy's harness, though, he frowned.

"I didn't expect you to bring a kindergarten along," he said to Lemel. "And a zoo," he added, noticing Goldie's traveling jam jar at Fishel's belt.

Sender said, "I'm sorry. I tried to explain to my mother, but she doesn't like excuses."

"My goldfish won't make any trouble," Fishel said. "He can't get out."

Another man got out of the car, an older man, with touches of gray in his hair. Unlike the property manager, who was now dressed in a T-shirt and jeans, this man wore a jacket and tie. "It's all right, Steve," he told the other man, "he has the little kid on reins, and I don't think anybody could object to a goldfish. I don't think there should be a problem."

Steve shrugged. "It's your house," he said. He turned to the boys. "This is Mr. Sterling. He owns the house. I don't actually know your names."

Lemel, Sender, and Fishel introduced themselves.

"Nice to meet you, boys," said Mr. Sterling. "When Steve phoned me to ask permission to take you all through the house, I was so interested in what he told me, I thought I'd come along, too. Most boys your age only think of vandalizing properties, but you sounded as if you'd appreciate it."

"I love the house!" said Lemel. "I wish somebody lived

in it. It's a shame to let it go like this."

"Yes, it is," Mr. Sterling agreed. "It belonged to my uncle, and he did live in it, but even then, he didn't seem to care about keeping it in good condition. And he certainly couldn't afford the servants it needed. You see, when houses like this were built, a hundred years ago or so, rich people had armies of servants to take care of the houses as well as the people who lived in them."

"What do you mean?" Lemel asked. "Roofers?"

"No, though they'd be needed now and then. People had to dust and sweep and straighten up, and clean out the fireplaces every day. And it was a lot dirtier in those days, too."

"The factories?"

"That's right. Whinbury was a mill town. It was famous for the smoke and dirt and the bad smells."

"Shall we get started?" asked Steve, jingling the keys. He opened the front door, but before letting any of the boys in, he said, "Stay close to me. Some of the floors upstairs are rotten, and downstairs here, a couple of big pieces of plaster decoration have fallen down. Don't even walk into a room if I don't." He turned to Sender. "And whatever you do, don't let go of your little brother," he ordered.

"I won't, but please don't get too close to him, either you or Mr. Sterling. He bites," said Sender.

Mr. Sterling drew away a little. "I generally like children," he said, "but..."

Sender laughed. "I know. I'm the only one who's safe. I understand."

CHAPTER 5

MR. STERLING'S PROBLEM

They all slipped in behind Steve. Inside, only little slices of light filtered through a few cracks in the boarded-up windows. In the dimness, the space around them seemed cavernous, and the men's footsteps echoed from the bare walls. The boys were all wearing rubber-soled shoes. Lemel was suddenly thankful that Steve had said the house wasn't haunted.

"Where's the switch, Steve?" Mr. Sterling's voice boomed in the emptiness. "I think I told you to leave the electricity on, didn't I?"

"Around here, somewhere." A moment later, Steve had switched on the lighting, but a single low-wattage bulb hanging from a length of electrical cord did little to brighten the hall they stood in. Mr. Sterling didn't seem to notice as he led the way to the two front rooms. Pushing the doors open, he felt around for the light switches, and turned on the bare bulbs.

Even from the doorway they could see that the room was huge. Everyone followed behind Steve as he walked further in.

"This one, here, with the big bay," Mr. Sterling said, "this was the drawing room. I guess people would have had parties here, but by the time I was old enough to visit, my uncle wasn't entertaining any longer." He walked toward a doorway within the first room. "If you go through here, you can see there are double doors that slide into the walls."

Leading them into the second front room, almost as enormous as the first, he went on, "This was the music room. My uncle used to have a grand piano in here. He had friends who played other instruments, and they used to get together and have informal concerts."

Walking through another door, they found themselves back in the entrance hall.

"Come see this," said Steve, pointing to a smaller room near the front door. "This is where they hung their coats. Imagine how many guests they could have!"

The boys crowded into the room.

Sender laughed. "The bedroom I share with my little brother would fit in here with space left over!"

Mr. Sterling laughed too. "You should see my tiny little apartment!" he said. He guided them past a grand staircase that led upstairs, and around toward a door at the side of the house. "This was the dining room." He threw the door open and flicked the switch.

Steve stopped the boys. "Just look from here," he said. "Some of the plaster decoration near the window has come down, and more is on the way."

Lemel gazed with awe at the huge chunk of plaster, the size of a microwave, that lay on the floor. Steve hadn't been kidding.

"It's the dampness," Mr. Sterling said sadly. "The rain comes in over the bay. It used to be so beautiful. There were drapes at the windows that must have cost a fortune, and there were two enormous Oriental carpets on the floor. The other rooms had Orientals, too, but I only remember the ones in the dining room. The chandeliers are gone, but even this little bulb will show you the fireplace. Every family room had a grand one, and every one was different. You can imagine the size of the dining room table. I never saw it full of people, though."

They walked to the back of the house, where they faced a row of normal-sized rooms along a hallway that ran across the whole house. "I don't even know what these rooms were for, but probably not for the family. The servants would have used them."

From the hallway, a modest staircase led down to the kitchen. There was a big room for the servants' dining room, a vast kitchen, and a lot of smaller rooms.

"Pantries and I don't know what else," said Mr. Sterling. "The service door is over there." He pointed to a short hallway to the back of the house.

"Is that what they called the tradesmen's entrance?" Lemel asked. He was a reader.

"That's right. Food and coal and things like that came to the back." Mr. Sterling smiled. "My uncle still had one servant, who cooked for him and took care of the few rooms he used. She must have been lost down here. Whenever I came, I used to slip down the stairs to see her. She always had something freshly baked for me. I think she was a bit lonely."

They trooped up the servants' staircase, which continued to the upper floors, but at the main landing, they went around to the grand staircase.

"We'll pretend we're family," said Mr. Sterling, "and use this one."

It led to a long half-landing with small rooms off it ("For personal maids and valets," said Mr. Sterling, "but two are bathrooms now"), and then up another few steps to a wide, full landing. Four enormous rooms opened off it. The landing itself was paneled in wood, with squares and rosettes at the corners where the squares met. The paneling surrounded a magnificent fireplace, with two statues supporting the marble mantelpiece.

Even with the bedroom doors open to let light in from the windows, and with the usual single bulb on, it was so dim that Fishel caught his foot in a hole in the worn carpet underlay that covered the floor.

"Watch yourself!" Mr. Sterling caught him. "I'm afraid the floors are all like this. I had to sell the carpets."

Walking into one of the grand bedrooms, he said, "This was Aunt Louise's room. Oh, you should have seen it! It was all white lace and frothy curtains, and it smelled of her perfume. She was a very grand lady, but she died long ago. My uncle outlived her by many years. She had very strong opinions." He laughed. "One of the front rooms used to be hers, but when the town put in streetlights, she said they bothered her so much she couldn't sleep, so she moved into one of these side rooms."

One flight up, the nursery floor brought back some sad memories to Mr. Sterling. "You see, my uncle was twenty years older than my mother, so his children were as old as uncles to me. I barely knew my cousins, but they had outgrown the nursery long before, anyway," he said. "They both died in the war. They were in the Royal Air Force, the RAF."

There was a long silence.

Steve took over the rest of the tour. They all followed him up to the next floor, with rows of smaller rooms for the servants. Then he led them up one more flight.

"This is the top floor," he said. "I think it was mostly for storage. Stay close to me. The roof's partly gone, and some of the floors are rotten. This room is interesting, though." He threw open a door to a very bright, sunny space. "See all the windows in the roof? They all open. Well, a lot of them are broken now, but you can imagine what they were like. Can you guess what they used this room for?"

Lemel looked around. "Sunbathing? Growing plants?"

Steve laughed. "Nothing so much fun. They dried laundry up here!" He pointed. "You can see where the floor's gone. Some of the other rooms here are just as bad." He let the boys look into the rest of the rooms, but only from the doorways. They were all empty and, aside from the drying room, not very big.

"Well, that's the lot," said Mr. Sterling.

As they returned to the ground floor, Lemel asked suddenly, "What happened to the furniture? Some of it might have been valuable."

Mr. Sterling shook his head. "I'm afraid it wasn't. My uncle seems to have thrown out all the old furniture when he redecorated between the wars. Everything was up to the minute in 1925, but by the 1960s it was just junk. Not like things made a hundred years earlier. And not of the same quality, though it was good. I sold it all, along with the chandeliers. I used some of the money to fix the worst holes in the roof, but I needed the rest to live on."

He looked around him at the shabby, torn floor coverings and peeling wallpaper. "It's a pity," he added, echoing the boys' thoughts. "I probably ought to sell the house, but I can't bring myself to. Anyone who bought it would just knock it down and build apartments. I only visited the house a few times when he lived here. I fell in love with it, but he didn't do me any favors when he left it to me. I can't even pay the taxes on it! I live in a little apartment in Bolton. The trouble is that my uncle used to tell me his investments would pay for the house, but when we looked at his accounts, we didn't find anything. I used to think he was some kind of miser, but now I think he was just dreaming."

"Maybe there was a hidden safe!" said Lemel.

"I wish!" Mr. Sterling gave a little sigh. "When I took the pictures off the walls to sell them, I was sure I'd find a safe behind one, but I didn't. There was absolutely nothing."

The boys all thanked Mr. Sterling for the tour. Then they filed sadly out the door and watched Steve lock up.

"Your little brother was as good as gold," said Steve to Sender.

"I guess he was as impressed as we were," Sender said. "It was really amazing!"

CHAPTER 6

WHAT'S AN OLIGARCH?

Suddenly, Mr. Sterling turned to the boys.

"You know, boys, Steve can only come in every two weeks, and then only for an hour or so. Would you be willing to keep an eye on the house for me, just look at it as you pass to see that nothing looks suspicious?"

"Sure!"

"Of course!"

"No problem!"

"Steve, do you have a business card on you?" Mr. Sterling asked.

"I always do," said Steve.

"Can you give them one?"

"I can give them three." Reaching into his pocket, Steve handed each boy a business card with his name and telephone number on it. "If you notice anything strange, give me a call right away, all right?"

"You know what?" said Mr. Sterling. "Show them where you keep the keys, Steve. I want them to be able to get into the house if they need to. They aren't the sort to make it into a clubhouse." He thought for a moment. "No, that's not fair. If you boys want to use the basement — you know, the servants' dining hall and the kitchens and so on — I don't see that it'll do any harm. It's only right, if I'm asking you to keep an eye on the house, to let you have some privilege in return."

Lemel, Sender, and Fishel exchanged looks of pure bliss. Nobody else in their cheder had ever earned a reward like this!

"We'll be really careful, Mr. Sterling," Lemel said seriously. "And we don't usually have time to come in, anyway. We're in school till six every day. But it's easy for us to take a quick look as we pass. It's on the way to school for all of us."

Sender said, "Would you mind if we looked around for a hiding place for money, Mr. Sterling? We'd like to help you. We wouldn't cause any damage."

Mr. Sterling thought about it. "The house is in such bad shape, anyway," he said. "I don't think you can hurt it much."

"Not at all!" said Fishel.

"Then I think Steve should let you use the keys whenever you like," Mr. Sterling decided. "I don't believe you'll find anything, but you'll have fun, and maybe I'll have a little hope." He smiled. It was a friendly, warm smile. "It would be just like a story if you did find something, wouldn't it?"

Steve's eyebrows rose almost into his hairline, but he led them into the garage. "These were stables once," he told them. "This part was the tack room. That's where they keep the saddles, harnesses, and other horse equipment. There's a little space in the wall, here." He showed them while putting the keys away.

The boys were silent as they watched the two men leave.

Then Fishel let out a sudden yell. "Wow! I think I'm dreaming!"

The boys went home walking on air.

∞

Naturally, the arrangement had to be a secret. They couldn't have other boys demanding to be let into an empty house that belonged to somebody else!

Besides, Rosh Chodesh was so soon that they only had one chance to go through the house again before cheder started. Lemel went to the garage and took the keys from their hiding place. He fitted the big key into the lock, turned it, and pushed the handle. With no trouble at all, the door opened.

"We're in!" he said.

The other two ran ahead, then, noticing that Lemel hadn't followed them, they stopped.

"It's all right," he said. "I want to see which keys on this ring fit which doors. You can go hunt for secret places." Methodically, he tried each key in the lock for each room. When he found one that fit, he put a tiny sticker on it. He had a whole pocketful of little round stickers in different colors.

Sender, who had Zevy along, went upstairs, but Fishel looked over Lemel's shoulder.

"What are the colors for?" he asked.

"Light colors are for the ground floor. Blue is front, yellow is side, green is back," Lemel said, pointing to each one. "The darker colors are for upstairs. I only have light and dark, so I'll just have to remember the ones for the floors further on. I'm using orange for side bedrooms because I don't have two shades of yellow. But at least I'll know which is which for the two main floors." He went back to trying keys, writing numbers on the stickers with a pen.

"Oh, I see," said Fishel. "All the small rooms at the back get a number. Are you numbering the doors?"

Lemel shook his head. "Mr. Sterling might consider it damage. I'm just remembering that I'm counting from right to left, like *lashon kodesh*."

Fishel nodded. "Have fun. I'm going up to the top floor."

All of them tried tapping walls and floors, but nothing sounded hollow anywhere. If there was a hiding place, it was well concealed.

When they had finished, they carefully locked the door and put the keys away.

"It's a pity we didn't find anything," said Sender.

"We can always try again," said Lemel. "I didn't think to feel up inside the fireplaces."

"My favorite part is the servants' hall," Fishel said as they walked down the driveway. "Did you see that the floor is stone? Even if we wanted to, we couldn't do any damage. We can have a lot of fun there this winter."

That gave them something to look forward to when the weather turned dark and rainy. With autumn and winter coming, it was wonderful to have something new and different ahead.

Just before cheder started again, an exciting rumor flew around the community.

"Have you heard what they're saying?" Lemel asked his friends. "A real Russian oligarch is coming to Whinbury!"

"A what?" Fishel asked.

"Is it a new kind of flu?" asked Sender.

"An oligarch is a very rich businessman. The ones from Russia are billionaires!" Lemel had listened carefully to his father's explanation.

"So what?" said Sender. "We never see the queen, we'll never see an oligarch."

"This one's Jewish," said Lemel.

"Ah." Fishel waved a hand. "Doesn't mean a thing. He probably knows as much about Yiddishkeit as Goldie."

"What's he coming here for, anyway?" Sender asked curiously.

"He wants to buy a soccer team," said Lemel.

When the others had finished laughing, Lemel said, "No, really, that's what they do. Arab sheiks and Russian oligarchs: they buy soccer teams. I think it's a prestige thing, for *kavod*."

"Well, we don't have a team to sell him, so I guess we won't see him," Sender said.

Lemel looked a little discouraged. "No, probably not. It would be fun, though."

CHAPTER 7

CRISIS

When school started again, the boys were too busy to think of oligarchs or even of exploring the servants' rooms in the old house. Their rebbe, Rabbi Bergman, was lively and interesting. He made learning exciting, and they felt they were *shteiging* with him.

"You really know the *parashah* well," Fishel's father said to him one Shabbos. "You answered every single question on the sheets perfectly! Chumash, *Mishnayos*... are you sure you aren't somebody else's son?"

Fishel laughed. He wasn't usually one of the best students. It wasn't that he played around, it was only that he didn't catch on as quickly as some others. But when he did catch on, it generally stayed.

"Somehow, when Rabbi Bergman explains things, they go right in!" he told his father.

"We really have to give Rabbi Bergman some kind of present," his mother said. "Fishel has never had a rebbe like him!"

Although Lemel and Sender were both quite good students, they also felt that they were learning better than ever before.

"You give the rebbe something in his *shalach manos*, don't you, Tatty?" Lemel asked his father.

"I do, and I know what you're going to say. We should put in a little extra this year, shouldn't we?"

Lemel certainly agreed.

For Sender, it wasn't so simple. His family didn't have a penny to spare. But to his relief, he found out that his father was so pleased with the amount of knowledge Sender was bringing home that he was writing thank-you notes every week to Rabbi Bergman. Sender's father taught in a different cheder, and he knew how much it meant to a rebbe to be appreciated.

"Money is very welcome," Sender's father told him, "but even a thank-you note shows Rabbi Bergman how much I appreciate his work."

One morning, Rabbi Bergman stood in front of the classroom, not saying anything but looking at the class. They wondered what was wrong. All of them began trying to remember what they had done in the last few days. Judging from the serious expression on Rabbi Bergman's face, it must have been awfully bad. But nobody could think of any misdeeds bad enough for the school to get involved.

Finally, Rabbi Bergman spoke. "I've been trying to

decide whether or not to tell you all about this," he said, "but I think you're responsible enough to understand, and maybe to help. The cheder is in a big financial hole. It needs hundreds of thousands of pounds to meet its bills. If we don't all help out in whatever way we can, Torah MiSinai may have to close."

Lemel held up his hand. "Why all of a sudden?"

"When the cheder was started, local *gevirim* donated property to the school. All the rents from those buildings went to help with the school budget. But a lot of the properties are in neighborhoods the city wants to redevelop. Does anybody know what 'eminent domain' means?"

Most of the boys shook their heads in bewilderment. Even Lemel, who usually knew the answers, was baffled.

"It's a law that lets the government take private property for public use, if the government gives fair compensation to the property owner. That means the owner has to sell to the city, whether he wants to or not. Then the city knocks the buildings down to build modern housing. The city doesn't pay much for the properties, certainly not what they're worth to the cheder. So the income that used to be the backbone of the finances of Torah MiSinai has suddenly dried up."

There was a silence. Eventually, Fishel asked, "What can we do?"

"I don't know. I hope some of you will have ideas. The parents are doing their best. I've heard they have some big plans. But I think you can contribute, too, in a smaller way. Do you think you can try?"

There was a chorus of agreement.

"Sure, Rebbe!"

"We'll think of things!"

"We have to!"

"Thank you, boys. Bring your ideas to me, and I hope we can find some that are workable." Rabbi Bergman sat down. "Now we can get on with the lesson."

Even though they were distracted by Rabbi Bergman's news, the boys did try to concentrate on learning, but it was awfully hard.

When he arrived home that evening, Lemel asked his father, "What are we doing for the cheder? Rabbi Bergman explained why the cheder has run out of money, and said all of us in the class could think of ways to earn some."

His mother came into the room in time to hear his question.

"We've formed a mothers' committee," she said. "We're going to have bake sales, and somebody is going to put on a play, and we're thinking of some kind of important evening affair."

"And the fathers," said Mr. Goldstein, "are organizing a big dinner with a brochure. We'll sell ads in the brochure. We're davening that all the businesses in town take really big ads. That's one way we'll raise money. And tickets to the dinner won't be cheap, either. A lot of fathers went to Torah MiSinai themselves, and they're really putting themselves out for it."

"I didn't know it was so old," said Lemel.

"It was the first real cheder in Whinbury," his father

told him. "Before that, there was a Jewish school, but it didn't allow much time for *kodesh*, and the *kodesh* standard wasn't high. Mr. Markovski — you know, the one who started Markovski's Groceries — he started the cheder."

"Wow, I didn't know that. So Mr. Markovski was a real pioneer!"

"He was, and his whole family has always supported the cheder. Some of his sons taught there, too."

"So the Rabbi Markovski who's the *menahel* is one of his sons?"

"That's right. The cheder is vital to the community."

"We've got to save it!" Lemel exclaimed.

In their own houses, Sender and Fishel were having much the same conversation. By the time they reached cheder the next morning, all three were determined to meet the challenge and find some way to earn money for the school.

Between Rabbi Bergman's wonderful lessons and the excitement of thinking of money-raising projects, the boys were so caught up that they half forgot about the old house. As the weeks passed, all the boys did was glance at it as they passed. Occasionally, one of them walked up the driveway and peered in the windows at the back.

Once the clocks changed and they were passing the house after dark, it was easier to tell if there were any lights in the rooms. Everything seemed fine.

"That's good," said Fishel. "We don't have to worry about the house. Now we can really concentrate on thinking of ways to save the cheder!"

A lot of the ideas boys proposed to Rabbi Bergman were really impractical, like opening a fair or starting businesses. One or two ideas were good, like having little neighborhood bazaars or yard sales. But as the boys who set them up found, they were a lot of work, and the money they brought in wasn't much. Not when you thought about thousands and thousands of pounds of debt.

CHAPTER 8

WHERE IS RABBI BERGMAN?

A week before Chanukah, they came to cheder on Sunday morning to find the *menahel*, Rabbi Markovski, teaching their class.

"I hope this is only a temporary arrangement," he told them. "Look, I'll be open with you. Rabbi Bergman has disappeared. He went to daven an early *shacharis* this morning, and hasn't been seen since. Nobody knows where he is. You can imagine that his wife is worried sick, and people are afraid that something has happened to him. It's been reported to the police, but their policy is that they won't take action for another day or two. So we're going to start the day by saying a *perek* of *Tehillim*."

There was a long, thoughtful silence.

A boy near Fishel raised his hand. "We like Rabbi

Bergman a lot," he said. "Shouldn't it be more than only one *perek*?"

There was a murmur of agreement from the class.

"We'll behave really well for you," another boy promised.

"All right," Rabbi Markovski agreed. "We'll make it two *perakim*. I don't know if I should take more time from lessons, though. You see, it may take a little longer for you to learn the same material when somebody else teaches you. Each rebbe has his own style."

The boys appreciated being treated like adults and told the truth about Rabbi Bergman. And behind their learning was the worry that he might be lost or hurt, with nobody knowing. It kept them from becoming too high-spirited. It stayed with them even after they finished cheder each day. So even though it was hard, and became harder as the days passed, they kept their promise to behave for Rabbi Markovski.

"He could be in a hospital with amnesia," said Lemel, "not knowing who he is," he explained.

"But a *frum* man looks so different, wouldn't somebody report it?" asked Fishel.

Sender agreed with him. "It's just so strange that he didn't come home from *shacharis*," he said. "My father says everybody saw him go out the door and turn down the street — and that was the last anybody knew."

Flyers were posted on lampposts and handed out in stores, asking anyone who had any information at all to tell the community *askanim* or the police, but no phone calls came in.

"It's scary," said Lemel. The others nodded.

Women who said *Tehillim* for people added Rabbi Bergman's name to their lists. Within a day, there were two gatherings in the community to say *Tehillim*, one for adults and one for children. Lemel, Fishel, and Sender went to the children's one (Sender's mother let him attend without Zevy). They recited *Tehillim* with more *kavanah* than they'd ever had before.

"It makes me feel shivery," Fishel confessed to the other two. "How can someone just disappear?"

The others nodded soberly.

At first, the police hadn't been interested, because they said people often just wandered off and eventually came home. They didn't understand that it was extremely unusual for *frum* people, especially one of the best rabbeim in the cheder, to do that. Even when they took the case seriously, though, they had no leads.

How do you track down somebody who vanishes into thin air?

Two days after Rabbi Bergman disappeared, Mr. Goldstein came home from *shacharis* full of news.

"You'll never guess who we had in my minyan!" he told Mrs. Goldstein.

"Who?" she threw over her shoulder. She was washing the previous night's supper dishes. She never really caught up on dish washing, but it didn't particularly bother her.

"Remember I told you a real Russian oligarch was coming here?" he asked.

"Yes..."

Lemel glanced up from his cornflakes. He was the only one up early. His sisters were between terms and taking advantage of the break to sleep late. "I remember. A Russian billionaire! You said one was coming to buy a soccer team. What was he doing in your minyan, Tatty?"

"Well, it seems it's not just any Russian oligarch. His name is Mikhail Berman. And the important fact is that he's a *baal teshuvah*!"

"You're joking!" laughed Mrs. Goldstein.

"No, really!" Mr. Goldstein assured her. "Tallis and tefillin and the lot. A crocheted yarmulke, but he's *frum*, all right." His expression changed. In a worried tone he added, "I just hope Putin doesn't turn on him. At the moment, they say he's a friend, but you know how fast things change there."

"Who's Putin?" asked Lemel.

Mr. Goldstein explained about the Russian government and that Putin was, for all intents and purposes, an absolute ruler. "But he can change his mind overnight and throw his ex-friends into jail."

"So it's not always good to be rich, I guess," said Lemel.

"It's hardly ever good to be rich," Mrs. Goldstein said as she went back to the dishes. "I ran into Mrs. Chaifetz, who used to live in that enormous house by the park, the Mrs. Chaifetz who moved away a couple of years ago, remember? She's back for a *simchah*, and she told me that when they lived here, her husband never got to eat a meal in peace."

Mr. Goldstein glanced up. "So maybe I shouldn't ask for a raise, after all," he said in mock seriousness.

Mrs. Goldstein laughed. "I don't think we're in line for problems like that. But how did you know you had a Russian millionaire — I mean billionaire — in shul with you?"

"He was surrounded by guards, great big hefty guys with body armor and bristling with weapons. They talked all through davening. In Russian."

"Wow!" said Lemel. "I can't wait to get to cheder to tell Fishel and Sender! Maybe we'll get to see an oligarch after all!"

"I'd rather see Rabbi Bergman," said Mr. Goldstein, sobering. "He means a lot more to all of us than somebody who wants to buy a soccer team."

"I wonder if anybody has news," said Mrs. Goldstein. "My ladies' group is still saying *Tehillim*."

"So are all the minyanim," added Mr. Goldstein. "Ask in class, Lemel. Maybe your *menahel* will have heard something."

But Rabbi Markovski had nothing new to report. There were still no leads. "All anybody knows is that it couldn't have been a car crash. Rabbi Bergman doesn't have a car," he told the boys.

At break time, Lemel had a chance to tell his friends about the visitor in his father's minyan. Their eyes lit up.

"I wonder how many guards he has!" said Fishel.

"Do you think they'll get him to give a talk?" Sender asked. "People are always interested in *baalei teshuvah*. And in Russians, too."

"And in oligarchs!" Fishel added.

"Maybe that could be our idea to raise money for the cheder!" Lemel exclaimed.

CHAPTER 9

FISHEL'S CLUE

But other people had the same idea, it turned out. By Tuesday afternoon, announcements were posted in many stores and in shuls, inviting people to a talk by the Russian billionaire in the biggest hall in the community, with the proceeds going to the Torah MiSinai fund. It was set for the last night of Chanukah.

The boys walked to cheder together on Wednesday morning and discussed the event.

"Top security!" Fishel said. "My mother says that women won't even be allowed to bring handbags into the hall!"

"I heard that no cell phones are allowed," said Sender.

"And they're going to have airport-style searches of

every person," Lemel added. "Do you think his guards will do the men? Real Russian thugs!"

When they reached cheder, they found Rabbi Markovski already in their classroom. As soon as he had taken attendance, he said, "Boys, Mr. Lieber has called in sick. He has the flu."

A chorus of *"Refuah sheleimah!"* interrupted him.

"Thank you, and I'll pass that on," said Rabbi Markovski. "But he obviously can't teach secular studies in the afternoon, and I can't find a substitute. I'm going to let you leave two hours early, until he recovers, as long as somebody is home when you get there. It will probably be for a week. If anybody has a problem with this arrangement, please see me after class."

Fishel cheered, and he wasn't alone. Who doesn't like to get out of school early?

Rabbi Markovski looked sternly over his glasses at him. "It's not very kind of you to cheer over somebody else's sickness!" he said.

Fishel looked apologetic, but he was still feeling good. For a boy who had to work harder than anybody else to do well, two hours fewer each day meant a lot!

At the end of classes, Fishel ran home feeling light and free. After greeting Goldie, he explained to his mother why he had come in early.

"Oh, dear! Poor Rabbi Markovski!" she said. "He must be feeling as stretched as a tight rubber band! But I'm glad you're home." She handed Fishel some money. "Do me a favor, and go to the bakery for a loaf of whole grain bread, please. I just noticed that we're almost out, and

I need to have some in stock for Tatty when he comes back. I'm in the middle of baking for Aunt Dena's kiddush, and I don't have time to go."

Fishel didn't mind. "Why the bakery?" he asked. "You always get bread at the kosher supermarket."

"They don't carry whole grain. It'll have to be the bakery."

Tucking the money away securely, Fishel put Goldie in its travel jar, tied the mesh bag to his belt, and set out.

The bakery wasn't crowded, and there was only one person ahead of Fishel. But from the way he talked, you would have thought he had nothing to do the whole day but chat about peculiar people he had met. The man behind the counter wasn't helping, either.

"We get some strange ones in here too," he said. "Just this week, some non-Jew has been coming in for bread and sandwiches. I never saw him before. He seems to be buying for someone else, because he always pulls out a list and checks everything against it. And when we didn't have one kind of sandwich and I told him he could get it in the grocery, he said his 'friend' said he had to buy it here."

"That *is* strange," the man in line agreed. "He could be a carer, though."

"No way. Nobody who looks like that goes into caring."

"What *does* he look like?"

The man behind the counter shrugged. "Shaved head. Nasty expression. He doesn't smile, and doesn't say please or thank you. Hoodie and sweatpants in a horrible color, a kind of orange, but not a healthy color. He never seems to change his clothes. That's another strange thing about him."

A brainwave hit Fishel like a sledgehammer. He had to talk to Lemel or Sender! Or preferably both!

Finally, the man finished. Fishel paid for the bread and dashed home, Goldie's jar bouncing against his hip. His mother was on the phone, so he wrote a quick note on a scrap of paper to tell her where he had gone, and ran off.

Sender lived nearby, but when Fishel got there, he was out. Fishel went on to Lemel's house, where he found both boys.

"We thought we could all go to the park before they lock it up for the night," said Sender when Fishel appeared.

"No! We have to go to the police!" gasped Fishel, out of breath from all the running. "I think I've found a clue!"

"A clue! Finally!" exclaimed Lemel.

"What is it?" Sender asked.

Fishel described what he had heard at the bakery. "And I suddenly thought," he went on, "what if Rabbi Bergman has been kidnapped?"

"But why should anybody want to kidnap a cheder rebbe?" Sender asked.

"And why hasn't there been a ransom note?" asked Lemel.

Suddenly, Fishel felt less enthusiastic. It had been such a good idea!

"I still think we should tell the police," he said stubbornly. "A non-Jew nobody knows, who buys from a list, who isn't a carer. Besides," he said, "you can buy kosher sandwiches anywhere. Every kosher grocery carries them. But the bakery is a little shop. People would notice somebody different coming in. In a grocery, he'd just be some local guy, or coming in with the workmen from the building project. What if that was the only way Rabbi Bergman could communicate? What if he hoped people would wonder why this strange guy was coming in and buying kosher food?"

Lemel and Sender thought about that. Eventually, Lemel said, "You've done some really deep thinking about this, Fishel. Maybe you have something. What do you think, Sender?"

"I think we ought to do as Fishel said. Go to the police. But it's not much, and they may not listen to us."

"I know, but at least we can try," said Lemel.

CHAPTER 10

A LIGHT IN THE WINDOW

Although there had been talk about closing the local police station, the move hadn't happened yet. The three boys climbed the steps to the door and slipped inside. None of them had ever been inside a police station. They looked around curiously, but there wasn't much to see. In front of them was a reception desk, with a glass partition to the ceiling. A hallway stretched down to the left. There was nothing else to look at. Except for a few "Wanted" posters and items of public information, the walls were bare, painted a faded green.

Nobody was at the desk, so Lemel pushed the button he saw there, labeled "Push for Service." A policewoman came through a door behind the partition.

"What do you kids want?" she asked. She wasn't

angry, only suspicious that three boys might have thought of a new way of being a nuisance to the police.

Sender and Fishel pushed Lemel forward. He was always neater than the other two, and his glasses gave him a responsible look.

"It's about Rabbi Bergman, who disappeared," he said politely. "We think we may have come across a clue."

The policewoman sighed. "You kids have been reading too many books. You'll be telling me about secret passages next." She leaned forward, elbows on the desk. "Look, do us all a favor and buzz off, okay?"

"Couldn't you just hear what we have to say?" Lemel begged. "As long as we know we've done the right thing by telling the police, we won't bother you."

The policewoman groaned. "More paperwork. Okay, go ahead." She poised a pen over a pad of paper.

Before beginning, Lemel thought for a moment to organize his ideas. "My friend Fishel Zillowitz heard something in the bakery," he began. The policewoman made him spell Fishel's name before going on. Then Lemel repeated what Fishel had overheard, and why he thought it was important.

"Kidnapping!" laughed the policewoman. "Does this rabbi of yours have money?"

"Probably not," said Lemel.

"Then why kidnap him?"

"We don't know, but we still think it's a pretty good theory," said Lemel stubbornly.

"I think you're imagining things. What can we do?"

"You could ask the baker to phone you next time

that man comes in, and then you could follow him," said Fishel.

"If we got there in time. And he might just go home." The policewoman was dismissive.

"Well, will you show the report to the sergeant?" Sender asked.

The policewoman rolled her eyes. "Will you go away if I promise to?" she asked.

"Only if we think you mean to keep your promise," said Sender sternly.

"All right, I'll show it to Sergeant Halesowen. I mean it. Even if it gets me into trouble. *Now* will you go?"

"I hope you're honest," said Lemel frankly. "After all, you do swear to uphold the law."

The policewoman put her head in her hands. "I'll do it, I'll do it! I promise on my honor as a police officer! Just leave, okay?"

As they walked back from the police station, the boys were silent. What good did it do to find a clue if nobody was interested?

"Could we follow him ourselves?" Fishel finally asked.

"I don't see how," said Lemel. "If the police won't listen, I bet the baker won't, either. So he won't phone us if the man comes in."

"Let's do something different to take our minds off this," Sender said. "Let's go look at the house, even though it's dark. Steve showed us the electricity was still on. We can go inside and hunt again for hiding places for that money."

"Good thinking!" the others approved. There was a pause.

"Uh, I hate to bring this up, but it's actually supper-time," said Fishel. "Maybe we should go later."

The other two were unhappy with the idea.

"What if my mother won't let me out?" asked Lemel. "She still seems to think I'm six."

"And I don't see how I can come if I have to schlep Zevy along," said Sender. "He really cramps my style."

"Why don't we just drop by the house for now, check that everything's all right, and then go home?" Lemel suggested. "It won't take more than an extra five minutes."

Fishel and Sender agreed, Fishel reluctantly (he was hungry), Sender happily.

They followed the street, walking from one pool of brightness under a streetlight to the next. Ahead of them, the huge house loomed, dark and mysterious.

"You're sure he said it wasn't haunted?" Sender asked.

"All he said was that he hoped it wasn't," Lemel said. "But right now we aren't going in, anyway."

They walked up the silent, overgrown driveway, under the leafless trees. The house's boarded-up windows stared blankly at the weedy lawn. The boys walked around to the back. Their feet crunched slightly on a patch of gravel around the back entrance, but the sound was muffled by the grass and weeds growing up through it. Everything was dark.

Lemel tried the back entrance, but it was locked. He

stepped back and scanned the upstairs windows. Still dark.

"Okay," he said, "we may as well go home."

He led the way back across the rear of the house and around to the side, between the old garage and the part of the mansion where the dining room bay bulged out. Here, too, he stepped back and looked up at the upstairs windows.

Suddenly, he grabbed Fishel's arm. "Look up there!" he whispered.

Fishel turned to Sender and pointed. There was just enough light from the streetlight for Sender to see his finger. All three boys turned their eyes upward.

"Am I imagining it?" Lemel asked. "It's not just the reflection of the streetlight, is it?"

"I see something, I think, just a little glow, like a candle," said Sender. "Is that what you're seeing?"

"Me too," said Fishel. "We can't all be seeing things."

"We've got to get to a phone!" Sender was almost shaking with excitement. "We have to call the property management agency!"

CHAPTER 11

A SHOCKING DISCOVERY

They ran to Sender's house, the nearest, but his sister was on the phone.

"She'll be on for hours," said Sender in disgust. "Forget it."

They ran on to Lemel's house. His mother was talking to someone on their phone, and seemed set for a long conversation, so they dashed to Fishel's house.

"My father's away. There's only me and my mother to use the phone," he panted as they plunged through the front door. "We ought to have a better chance."

Sure enough, the phone was free. Fishel ran up to his room to get Steve's business card. He handed it to Lemel, but Lemel handed it back.

"It's your phone," he said. "You get to call."

"I don't know what to say," said Fishel, passing the

card back. "You do it."

Sender nodded his agreement. Lemel stabbed the buttons with decisive fingers. He held the phone to his ear, then, after a while, slowly put it down.

"What's wrong?" Sender asked.

"It just rang and rang. It didn't even take a message," Lemel said. "I'm not sure what to do now."

"What are you boys muttering about?" asked Fishel's mother. "You sound like you're plotting to overthrow the government." Without waiting for an answer, she added, "Your supper's ready, Fishel," and, turning, went back to the kitchen.

Fishel shrugged. "I'm pretty hungry," he said. "Tell me later what you decide to do next." He followed his mother.

Lemel and Sender looked at each other.

"It isn't as much fun without all of us together," Sender said.

They let themselves out of the house and walked home to have supper. Lemel was so distracted that he didn't even notice that it was cheese casserole, which he hated.

After supper, he called Sender, and actually got through. "Can we go now?" he asked. "It's not even seven yet."

"I'll try. I'll meet you there if I can get out. I'll bring a mini flashlight. Have you asked Fishel?"

"No, I'm calling him next."

Lemel hung up and dialed Fishel's house. Fishel answered. "I've already asked. My mother says I can go, but only for an hour," he said.

"It shouldn't even take that long," said Lemel. "I'll meet you there. Bring a small flashlight." He hung up.

The three boys walked quietly up the weedy drive and stood in a patch of shadow near the garage. They stared at the window where they had spotted the glow, but it was as dark as the rest of the house.

"What are you planning to do?" Fishel asked Lemel in a low voice.

"I don't really know. First I want to unlock the back door and get in. It's farthest from the room with the light, so if we make any noise, I hope whoever is there won't hear it. We need to see if anybody is in that room."

"If they're vandals, they may be big guys," said Sender. "We'd better be really careful."

"How can we stop them?" Fishel worried.

"We can't," said Lemel, "but once we see what's going on, maybe we'll think of something. And I'll try Steve again tomorrow."

He took the keys from their hiding place in the garage.

"Do you want to lead, Sender?"

Sender nodded eagerly. This was his opportunity to do something important!

They descended the steps to the tradesmen's entrance. Lemel unlocked the door and backed away to let Sender go ahead of him.

Sender squared his shoulders and whispered, "All right, men, let's go!"

Closing the door behind them, the three boys quietly

made their way through the basement rooms. Only Sender switched his flashlight on, his fingers over the light so it gave no more than a faint glow. They tiptoed through the darkness, grateful there was no furniture to trip over. When they reached the staircase, they kept close to the banisters to avoid creaks.

They had only climbed to the main floor when they heard the back door open. Low, angry voices came to them.

"You didn't lock it!"

"I did! I know I did!"

"You seem to know a lot, but the door was still unlocked!"

There was a brief scuffle, then footsteps began to come up the stairs. In a minute, the boys would be trapped!

Sender looked around frantically. The row of small back rooms was close by. He jerked his head to the nearest, and all three of them whisked inside. If only the strangers didn't think to look around. The boys held their breath.

Into Lemel's mind came all the stories he'd read of people hiding, given away by a sneeze. *Please, no sneeze!* he thought, then felt an urge to laugh at the silly rhyme. He bit the inside of his cheek hard to stifle the impulse. The other boys' breathing was shallow and quiet.

The strangers went on up the rear staircase to the next floor, where the bedrooms were. The boys breathed again. They had a hasty whispered consultation.

"We have to follow them," said Sender.

"Yes, but I think only one of us should," Lemel said.

"Me!" said Fishel. He grinned. "If they spot me, I can just turn sideways."

The others agreed, and Fishel crept up the next flight of steps. Silently, he sidled past the row of small rooms and up the short flight to the upper landing.

The door to the side bedroom stood open, and the light was on. The small bulb gave very little light, but he could just make out one of the strangers. Fishel caught his breath. It was the man in the orange jogging outfit! He had been right!

About to go down to his friends, he hesitated. One of the men was speaking.

"So now we've got two of you," he said. "You're not worth anything. I'm trying to decide what to do with you." He was obviously talking to only one of a pair of captives.

"Do you think they got our ransom note?" asked the other thug. "We haven't heard from them. I think that's kinda funny."

"They're probably trying to figure out a way to catch us when they pay the ransom," said the first. "They'll never do it. I've got all the safeguards in the world. But I'm thinking about moving them, anyway. Just in case."

"I still don't understand why you think anybody I know has money," said one of the captives. Fishel knew that voice. It was Rabbi Bergman!

"Ah, be quiet. You've been telling us the whole time we've got the wrong guy, but you haven't convinced us yet."

"Because you can't spell!" snapped Rabbi Bergman. "I know who you want: that Russian oligarch, Berman. But I'm Bergman!"

"I told you to be quiet. Or else!"

Fishel felt sick. Poor Rabbi Bergman!

CHAPTER 12

NO ONE TO TELL

Fishel eased away and tiptoed down the steps. Beckoning the other two out of the room, he led the way down to the basement and out again.

They left the door unlocked.

After Lemel put the keys back, Fishel told the others what he had heard. "Now I understand what's going on," he said, keeping his voice down.

"Yes," Lemel replied. "They snatched Rabbi Bergman by mistake. They'd never have gotten past those hulking Russian guards. I guess they're too dumb to realize that somebody without guards was the wrong person."

"And you were right, Fishel!" whispered Sender. "The only thing Rabbi Bergman could do to get some kind of message out was to tell the thug he had to have kosher food from only one place — the bakery. Just as you said, a shop small enough for a stranger to be noticed. Now we really have something to tell the police!"

"If they listen," said Lemel. "Do we have time to try again? My mother told me to be back by eight."

"We may just make it," said Sender, "if we run."

They pounded up the station steps and pushed through the door. A man was on duty this time. He looked down his nose at them.

"Are you the three nuisances who were in yesterday?" he asked.

"We're the same boys, but we have something concrete to tell you," Lemel said, pushing his glasses up and trying not to notice his heart sinking.

"I don't care if it's made of granite, I'm not having you waste my time. Don't you know wasting police time is a criminal offense?"

"We're not wasting it, sir, we have important information to give you," Lemel persisted.

"If it's as ridiculous as a guy in a bakery, you can leave. Now. Beat it. Scram." The policeman leaned over the desk. "You heard me!"

The three boys looked at each other and shrugged. They went slowly down the steps to the street.

"Well, I guess it's up to us, then," said Lemel.

"We can have a conference in our sukkah — I mean my family's sukkah. It's still up," said Fishel. "My father was talking about taking it down, but he won't be home till the end of the week. It's all ours."

"You two can meet. I have to go home," Lemel said disgustedly, checking his watch. "I have four minutes."

"No, we'll talk right after school," Sender said. "We've still got those extra two hours. I hate to leave Rabbi Bergman with those thugs, but maybe we'll think of something overnight. And I'll have to think of an excuse not to drag Zevy along. My mother said as long as I was getting out of school early, I had to take Zevy for a walk every day. So I have to go straight home from cheder. I can come to Fishel's place afterward."

The extra time for thinking was no help at all. As soon as they gathered in Fishel's sukkah, they all admitted that they had no ideas.

Even worse, Sender was schlepping Zevy.

"This isn't something kids should be doing," Lemel said. "We really ought to ask our parents what to do."

Fishel sighed. "My father's still out of town. I don't want to worry my mother while he's away."

"Who else is there?" Lemel asked. "We can't bother Rabbi Markovski. He's already going crazy, losing two teachers at once."

"Why can't you ask your parents?" asked Sender.

"I don't think they'd understand," Lemel said heavily. "They always seem to think I can't tell imagination from reality. What about yours?"

"Don't look at me," said Sender. "My mother's out at a meeting, and my father has a *chavrusa*. Last time they were both out I called them so many times, I'm not allowed to interrupt them any longer. There's only the babysitter, and I'm sure not going to ask her!"

"What if they move Rabbi Bergman while we're waiting?" Fishel demanded.

Lemel thought for a moment. "I remember when I was reading *The Rooftop Mystery* last summer," he said, "my father said that children shouldn't be doing the work of the police. So I asked him what if the children told the police and the police didn't do anything? He said they'd done their duty by reporting the incident."

"That's no use! We can't just leave Rabbi Bergman!" Fishel protested.

They all agreed that it was out of the question.

"It looks as though we're going to have to take care of this ourselves," Lemel said. "I really, really don't like it. We'll just have to be awfully careful. And having Zevy along isn't a good idea, Sender."

"I tried," Sender said. "I really tried. I told my mother there might be trouble, but she didn't even listen. She just told me not to argue with her. She said he'd bitten her twice today and she wasn't looking for a third time, and to get him out of the house."

Zevy gave everyone an angelic smile. Then he lunged at Fishel. Sender caught him just in time. "He ought to know not to try to bite you, Fishel," he said. "You're all bone. But I don't want to let him, anyway."

"Neither do I!" said Fishel, edging his plastic chair further away. "Maybe he should try to bite Goldie," he added. "Through the jar, I mean."

The jam jar was tied securely to his belt, but there was an enormous length of cord attached, which he had wound around his waist.

"What's all the rope for, Fishel?" Lemel asked.

"Well, I didn't want Goldie to miss the excitement,

and I figured if I could hang the jar from something, he'd have a good view," said Fishel simply.

"I hope there isn't going to be any excitement," said Lemel. "I guess we better get going. Do we all have flashlights?"

The other two showed theirs. Fishel's was a great big automotive flashlight. Sender had a tiny LED flashlight. Lemel had the same. He didn't tell the others that he also had his father's utility knife in his pocket. He was afraid it might be needed, but he didn't want to worry them.

"I guess we're ready, then," he said.

When they reached the house, they cautiously walked around it to check all the windows. No light showed.

"I think we're all right," Lemel said, and fetched the keys.

"Can we turn the lights on, then?" Sender asked.

"No, but you can use flashlights," Lemel said after a moment's thought.

The boys climbed the stairs and headed for the bedroom Fishel pointed out to them.

"That's Mr. Sterling's aunt's bedroom," he said, remembering. "I wonder if it smells of her perfume any longer."

"After all these years?" Sender snickered. "With luck, it'll smell of kosher sandwiches."

The door was unlocked.

Lemel waved at Fishel. "You were the spy. This is your reward. If you want it."

"What, to go first?" Fishel whispered. "You bet!"

He turned the handle and opened the door. They swept the room with their flashlights until the beams picked out Rabbi Bergman and Steve the property manager in one corner, both of them bound and gagged.

Lemel felt sick at seeing Rabbi Bergman tied up. He ran to untie Rabbi Bergman's gag and cut the ropes, while Fishel went to Steve. Sender hung back, trying to control Zevy and wishing his little brother were a thousand miles away. Babysitting was making him miss half the excitement!

"What are you doing here?" said Rabbi Bergman to the boys as soon as he could talk. "Get out of here before those thugs come back!"

"We'll explain later," said Lemel, sawing away at the ropes on Rabbi Bergman's wrists. "They're not here now, and this should only take a few minutes."

Fishel, too, pulled a pocketknife out of his pocket. "It's a good one," he told Steve as he untied the gag. "It'll cut through your ropes in seconds."

"You kids have to get away!" said Steve. "These men are dangerous!"

"We know," said Sender, who hadn't brought a knife. He was kicking himself. Why hadn't he guessed that the men might have tied up their prisoners?

And those thugs might come back any minute!

CHAPTER 13

SPECIAL WEAPONS

The boys worked away at the ropes. Sender hooked Zevy's reins over the door handle and ran to help untie the ropes as soon as the first one was cut. All of them kept listening for the kidnappers' return. Lemel could see that being on their guard was slowing them down, so he sent Sender and Zevy out of the room to keep watch.

At last, both men were free, but they were so stiff from being tied up that they could hardly walk.

"I'm sorry, boys," said Rabbi Bergman, "I can't get down those stairs yet. They did untie me to let me daven while they guarded me, but then they always tied me up again."

"We're still safe," said Lemel, "but if they come back—"

Just then, Sender tiptoed in. "I think I heard the

door," he whispered. "Flashlights out."

The room was plunged into darkness again.

"I hope they didn't spot the flashlights," Lemel whispered back. "Look, you two help Rabbi Bergman and Steve into one of the other rooms."

Downstairs, a light went on.

"Hurry!" whispered Fishel.

Footsteps sounded on the uncarpeted stairs.

By the time the kidnappers reached the half-landing, the boys had just managed to get the two prisoners into a front bedroom before dashing into two other rooms, hoping that if one of them was discovered, the others might escape. Lemel eased the door of the prison room shut and hid in the other side bedroom.

The light on the landing was switched on. Peering through doors opened only a crack, the boys saw the two kidnappers walk toward the bedroom where their captives had been held. The better-dressed one turned the handle, switched on the light — and stopped dead.

"They're gone!" He rounded on the sweat-suited thug.

"Didn't I tell you to tie them up whenever you're not here?" he demanded.

"I did! And I gagged them too!" Sweat Suit defended himself. He went over to the piles of ropes and examined them. "Hey, these have been cut! Come here and look for yourself, Vic!"

The other kidnapper stayed where he was. "We haven't been away for long," he said. "Search the place. They may still be here!" He turned.

Suddenly, Zevy coughed.

Lemel groaned to himself. Just what he was afraid of!

The kidnapper ran toward the bedroom Sender was hiding in and threw the door open. "Kids!" he exclaimed. "That's all we need. More prisoners. Come out here, you kids!" He stooped down a little to catch them.

Sender emerged. Zevy shot ahead of him, pulling the reins out of his hands. "No, Zevy! Come back here!" Sender shouted.

But Zevy was free at last, and even in the dim light of the landing bulb, he could see an uncovered arm. With a sweet smile on his adorable face until the last second, he dashed for Vic's arm and sank his teeth into it.

"Zevy! No! *Treif!*" Sender yelled.

For an instant, Zevy relaxed his grip, but the arm didn't move away fast enough. His teeth sank in again, further up.

Vic was yelling more loudly than Sender. "Get him off! Get him off!" He pushed at Zevy, but Zevy's jaws were pretty strong.

Sweat Suit came charging out of the bedroom, only to be met by Fishel, racing up the steps from the half-landing, swinging Goldie's jar around his head and shrieking like a banshee. Sweat Suit tried to dodge, but Fishel only let the cord out a little further.

"Are you crazy, kid?" Sweat Suit yelled.

Lemel took charge. "Drive them into that bedroom!" he shouted.

Fishel moved forward, still swinging Goldie in the jar. Sweat Suit backed up.

Holding Zevy's reins again, Sender pulled at Zevy.

"Let him go, Zevy," he said. "Do you want Mommy to give you a spanking?"

Zevy's jaws opened. Vic dodged away from the toddler, but Sender advanced. "Get in that room or I let him bite you again!"

Vic looked around wildly, but with Fishel blocking the stairs, he had no escape.

He looked at Zevy with horror. "That kid's a cannibal!" he whispered, his eyes wide with fear. He backed unwillingly toward Mr. Sterling's aunt's bedroom, only to collide with Sweat Suit, escaping from the menace of Goldie in the jar. They fought each other to get through the doorway.

"All the way in," said Lemel grimly.

The men took three steps further.

Lemel seized the door and, slamming it shut, slipped the marked key on his ring into the lock and turned it.

The kidnappers were captured!

"We're not going to waste time going to the police ourselves," said Lemel. "We'll have to get a grown-up. Sender, is your father home yet?" He knew Fishel's father wasn't due till late that night, so it was only a choice between his and Sender's fathers.

"I don't think so. He said he had to buy wicks for the menorah after he finished teaching."

"Then you and Zevy will have to stand guard. They may try to bash the door down," said Lemel. "Fishel, can you watch outside to make sure those guys don't escape through the window?"

"Sure, but it's a fifteen-foot drop!"

"They could tie the pieces of rope together. If you see them get out, either yell, or threaten them with Goldie, or at least make sure you see which direction they've gone in. I'll run home to tell my father."

"What about Rabbi Bergman and Steve?" Fishel asked.

"Leave them for now. By the time they're recovered, I hope the police will be here. I wish they'd leave, though. It still isn't safe. What if those two thugs break out?"

He dashed down the stairs, sweeping his flashlight across the steps to be sure of his footing.

Fishel ran after him to take up his post under the side window.

Steve limped out of the front bedroom he and Rabbi Bergman had been hidden in. "You kids are amazing!" he said, turning to Sender. "We heard it all!"

Sender shrugged. "I'm going to be in big, big trouble when my mother hears about all this," he said. "And I think I'm going to have to wash my little brother's mouth out with kosher soap, too. Maybe you and Rabbi Bergman should go, though. Those guys could break down the door and get out."

CHAPTER 14

CALL FOR HELP

Rabbi Bergman appeared, still looking a little shaky. "We can't possibly leave you boys here alone! We'll have to take our chances. I'm feeling a lot better now. Is there anything here we can use as a weapon?"

"Probably not," said Sender. "The house seems to have been cleared out right to the walls. We've been through it. I still have Zevy, though."

"What about Fishel? Does he still have that jam jar?"

"Yes, but he'll need it if they get out through the window."

There was an ominous thump against the bedroom door.

"I'm still here," Sender yelled. "With my brother!"

There were no more thumps for a while. He heard

Fishel shout from outside. He couldn't make out the words, but he guessed Fishel was also telling the kidnappers that he was on guard.

The minutes crawled. All at once, Sender lifted his head. "I think I hear a siren!" he said.

"Probably just a fire engine somewhere," said Steve gloomily.

"But maybe not," said Rabbi Bergman. He stumbled back into the front bedroom Lemel had pushed him into, and looked through the window. He thought he could see a blue light. "I think it is the police!" he said over his shoulder. "Yes, I can hear the siren now, and the light is coming this way! Steve — you haven't been tied up for as long as I have. You're not as stiff. Can you go to meet them?"

"Sure. I only hope they left an outside door open."

Sender caught his breath. "Lemel has the keys! What if the police can't get in?"

Rabbi Bergman laughed, a little unsteadily. "Lemel and Fishel had to get out somehow. I'm sure they were in too much of a hurry to lock the door behind them!"

Sender let his breath out. "Oh, right," he said. "Come to think of it, how did the kidnappers get in, in the first place?"

Steve looked embarrassed. "My guess is that Mr. Sterling's uncle's housekeeper used to keep a spare key under a brick or a flowerpot, the way they always do in books. I never thought to search – but the kidnappers must have."

Rabbi Bergman looked through the front window

again. "Yes, they're here!" he said.

"And here they come," said Steve, as light flooded the staircase and heavy feet pounded up the steps, big flashlights shining ahead of them.

Two police officers appeared, with Fishel on their heels.

"What's going on, here?" the first officer demanded.

"Kidnapping," Sender said briskly. "We have the kidnappers locked inside that bedroom." He pointed. "As soon as my friend gets back here, we can let them out."

"You called out the police for a *kids' game?*" roared the policeman. Sender recognized him. He was the policeman on desk duty who had sent them away the second time.

"No, officer." Rabbi Bergman limped forward. "I've been held for five days, and Steve here has been trapped for two."

"Who are you?"

"Rabbi Bergman."

"What, the guy who disappeared? Prove it." The police officer wasn't taking anybody's word for anything.

Rabbi Bergman fumbled in an inside pocket and pulled out a wallet with a credit card he never dared to use, and a family train pass. "Do these help?" he asked.

The policeman eyed them doubtfully. "Nothing with your picture?"

"I never carry my passport when I'm being kidnapped," said Rabbi Bergman, losing patience.

"Look, officer, I'm Steve Bateman," Steve intervened.

"Here's a business card. You can call my property office anytime. They'll get one of the partners to call you back."

"What are you doing here?"

"I came to check up on the property. It's my job. The thugs caught me and held me along with Rabbi Bergman. Maybe you should call your sergeant."

Lemel and his father came dashing up the stairs.

"Rabbi Bergman!" his father exclaimed. "Lemel wasn't kidding! We've all been saying *Tehillim* for you!"

Lemel looked indignant. Kidding! What did his father think he was, a five-year-old who couldn't tell fantasy from reality?

"Mr. Goldstein!" Rabbi Bergman greeted him. "You're a sight for sore eyes, but not as much as your son and his friends." He turned to the policeman. "These three boys found us and released us and even managed to catch the kidnappers."

"So where are they?" demanded the policeman. The second officer was beginning to look uncomfortable at his superior's continuing rudeness.

Lemel held out the bunch of keys. "I'll unlock the door, but be ready to grab them," he said. "They're pretty angry."

"Are you telling me my job?" Officer Number One scowled furiously.

"Maybe we should let the boys tell us in their own way," Officer Number Two suggested hopefully, but Officer One ignored him.

"Well, use the key then!" he ordered.

Lemel unlocked the bedroom door and quickly stood

back. Fishel stood ready, swinging the jam jar gently.

For a moment, nothing happened. Then the door flew inward, and the two men burst out — into Officer Two's arms.

"Well, what have we here?" he said jovially. The other officer scowled some more.

The thugs sagged. They were caught red-handed!

The second policeman glanced over his shoulder. "Are you accusing these guys of something?" he asked Rabbi Bergman.

"Yes! Kidnapping!"

"They kidnapped me too!" said Steve. "They tied us up and gagged us. The cut ropes are in the room, there."

"Good enough." The two policemen snapped handcuffs on both thugs. The men didn't resist.

"Just keep those kids away from us!" said Vic. "One of them bites, and the other one swings a jam jar!"

"They're deadly!" Sweat Suit agreed.

Fishel hurriedly hooked Goldie's jar onto his belt again and wound the cord around his waist.

Sender edged away with Zevy. "I'd better get home," he said. "My mother will be wondering where I am."

"If you get into trouble, tell her to call me — oh, but I don't know when the police will let me go home," said Rabbi Bergman. "They'll probably want a statement. Maybe later tonight."

"Thank you, Rebbe!" Sender dragged Zevy to the stairs and disappeared.

"Hey!" the first officer called. "We'll need a statement from you too!"

But it was too late. Sender was gone.

"It's all right, officer, you can go to his house. He has to take his little brother home, but when he tells his mother why he's late, she won't let him out of the house again," Lemel explained. "Fishel and I can go with you now, if you let us call home from the police station."

"We only have the one police car," growled the first officer, "and we need that for these thugs."

"Can you walk to the station from here?" asked the second policeman.

"I think you'd better take Rabbi Bergman in the car," said Lemel. "He's still pretty stiff. What about you?" he asked, turning to Steve.

"I can probably make it," said Steve. "It's not far to the station."

"I'll help you," said Mr. Goldstein. "I'm definitely coming along. It's a disgrace that the police ignored these boys, and I'll be putting in a complaint — and following up on it, too."

CHAPTER 15

LEMEL'S IDEA

Mr. Goldstein was still steaming when they all reached the station. When the policewoman (she was back on duty again) ignored the boys and asked him what he wanted, he leaned over the desk and glared at her.

"I want to make a complaint," he said, "and you're on my list, miss. Who's in charge here?"

"Sergeant Halesowen, but you can't see him," she said, edging back a little. Working for the police had toughened her up, but she wasn't used to seeing an Orthodox Jewish man being anything but perfectly polite.

"Why not? Is he invisible?"

Fishel and Lemel snickered.

"You have to have an appointment," the woman officer said firmly.

"Does he make an appointment before he makes an arrest? Do criminals book with him in advance?" Mr. Goldstein demanded. "Your service has put three little boys and a toddler at risk!"

"Oh, come now," said the woman.

"Let me tell you, *officer*," snapped Mr. Goldstein, "that because you and another *officer* ignored important information these boys had for you, they actually found two kidnapped men and captured the kidnappers by themselves. If you don't think that's dangerous, I do!"

"They shouldn't have done it themselves!" the woman protested. "That's what the police are here for!"

"But they couldn't get you to act! And I'm going to complain, and I'm going to take it right up to the police commissioner if I have to, and I'm going to make sure the careers of two incompetent police officers are stopped in their tracks! Do you understand me, madam?"

The woman took a form from a shelf behind her and pushed it toward Mr. Goldstein. "You have to fill out a form," she said faintly.

"Not till I've spoken to your Sergeant Halesowen! And I'm not moving from here till I do!"

"Neither are we!" said Steve. Rabbi Bergman nodded emphatically.

"Well, of course, you two gentlemen have to make a report," said the woman.

"We only speak to the sergeant," said Steve, as stubbornly as Mr. Goldstein.

In the end, everybody had the chance to speak to Sergeant Halesowen, because none of the adults would have anything to do with any other officer. First the boys were called to have their statements taken.

"You go first," Fishel whispered to Lemel. "I don't know anything about this."

"Neither do I!" Lemel protested, but he went first anyway, pushing his glasses up nervously.

"You just sit there, Mister Leemel Goldstein," said Sergeant Halesowen, "and the officer over there will write down what you say. Then you read it through and make any changes you think are needed, and then you sign it."

Lemel sat down in a chair facing the sergeant and explained the events as clearly as he could. To one side, he could see the officer's pencil racing across the paper. Now and then he remembered to slow down to let the officer catch up.

"And then the police came up the stairs," he finished. "I guess you know the rest."

"I wish more witnesses could give their reports like you," Sergeant Halesowen admitted.

Lemel read through the notes, corrected the timing in one or two places, and signed each page as he was told.

"Not so bad," he said to Fishel as he came out. "Just tell them what happened. Don't leave Goldie out either."

"How could I? Goldie is a hero!" Fishel retorted, and followed the officer in to Sergeant Halesowen.

When he had finished, Mr. Goldstein said, "Fishel, Lemel, go home now. I'll wait while they take statements from Rabbi Bergman and Steve, and then I'll take care of my business with them. Lemel, tell Mommy I may be home late."

The boys left.

It was after nine when Mr. Goldstein came home to tell Lemel what had happened.

"I won't go into details, but I made myself clear," he said. "If I don't get a formal apology — and the other two families, too — I intend to take it higher and, if necessary, give the story to the news. I may do that anyway. I still get cold shivers when I think about what could have happened."

"Sender says his mother is saying she'll never let him out after dark again," said Lemel, who had been using the phone fairly heavily. "And Fishel — his mother is even talking about a guard dog! With her allergy!"

Mrs. Goldstein said, "I think we'll all calm down after a while, but it certainly hasn't been a good experience. Bed now, Lemel. We'll keep you updated if anything else happens."

∞

Over the next few days, the boys learned that Rabbi Bergman had been told to take time off until the end of Chanukah, to recover.

"I'm just so glad we found him before Shabbos and before Chanukah," said Sender. "Imagine if he'd had to spend Shabbos tied up, and he couldn't have managed to light Chanukah candles at all."

"I don't even want to think about it," said Lemel. His

stomach felt as though a stone was lying in it. "We rescued him in time, *baruch Hashem*. That's all I want to remember."

"Me too," said Fishel. "But you know, Chanukah starts tomorrow night, so we'll get out of cheder early. That's what I'm thinking of!"

"And there's that talk that Mr. Berman is going to give!" Lemel remembered. "I hope they let us go. What if it's for grown-ups only?"

"Does he even know anything about this whole kidnapping business?" asked Fishel.

"I'll ask when I get home," Lemel said. "My parents seem to be pretty involved in all these plans."

The next morning, on the way to cheder, Lemel dropped his bombshell. "Not only does Mr. Berman know about the kidnapping, he wants to hear all about it from us!" he said.

"Us?" Sender's voice squeaked with shock. "He wants to talk to us?"

"That's right. He knows that Rabbi Bergman was kidnapped by mistake, and that the kidnappers were really after him," said Lemel. "He's impressed with us. Apparently, he thinks highly of our...our...uh, initiative and courage."

Fishel grinned. "I like compliments."

"My father said Mr. Berman was really apologetic. The kidnappers sent the ransom note to his hotel, but he thought it was some kind of silly joke and just threw it out. Now he wants to give Rabbi Bergman some money to make up for everything."

"That's awfully nice of him!" Sender said. "After all, it wasn't his fault at all."

"Except for chucking the ransom note. But anybody would have thought it was just some nut sending it," said Fishel.

They had nearly reached Torah MiSinai when Lemel stopped short. "Wait a minute," he said. "We get to talk to him, right?"

"I guess so," said Sender.

"Has he bought that soccer team yet?"

"How should I know?"

"What does that have to do with anything?" Fishel chimed in.

Lemel smiled mysteriously. "Never mind," he said.

The other two boys looked at him curiously, but he said nothing more.

CHAPTER 16

A GOODBYE PARTY

The Goldsteins had just finished lighting Chanukah candles when the phone rang. Lemel's mother took it, and then, with a mystified expression, she held it out to Lemel. "It's for you."

"Me?"

It was Steve.

"I've got some bad news for you," he said. "When Mr. Sterling heard what happened, he told me he can't have the house standing empty any longer. He's worried it will be used by other criminals. He's going to put it up for sale."

"Oh," said Lemel in a small voice. "That's really sad."

"The land is worth a lot. Mr. Sterling won't have to pinch pennies," said Steve.

"I know, but it's horrible that he has to give up the house," said Lemel.

"Well, anyway," Steve went on briskly, "Mr. Sterling said he wanted you boys to join him for a goodbye party in the house on Sunday. How does that sound?"

"Would he come at night? Like after supper?" asked Lemel, thinking of Chanukah lighting. "We could bring food and make it a real party. We'd all like to see him again."

"Let's make it at seven in the evening, okay? If there's a problem, I'll get back to you, but if you don't hear from me, consider it confirmed."

"I'll tell Sender and Fishel," said Lemel, trying to feel cheerful.

Steve hung up.

All the boys' parents agreed to the party, though Mr. Goldstein joked that maybe they should borrow one of Mr. Berman's Russian guards — just in case.

The boys reached the old house in plenty of time.

Mr. Sterling arrived promptly. As he got out of his car, he asked the boys to help unload. "I brought some things for the party," he said. "Not food, I know you only eat special food. Other things."

"We brought treats for everybody in Sender's father's wheelbarrow," said Lemel. "There's plenty."

When Mr. Sterling opened the house and turned on the lights, he said, "Shall we have our party in the living room or the music room?"

"Could we have it in the servants' hall?" Fishel asked. "There's a stone floor there. If we spill, it won't matter. And there's probably somewhere I can put Goldie so he has a good view."

"Sounds fine to me."

They all trooped down the servants' staircase with the boxes from Mr. Sterling's car and then again with all the party food. While they were bringing the food, Mr. Sterling was unpacking his boxes.

And what a collection he had! Party hats and horns and exploding confetti. A couple of silly games. Face paints. Balloons and a balloon pump. Brightly colored paper plates and paper napkins and cups. A dozen squat candles gave extra light. And — they all gaped — from the last big box, Mr. Sterling took out four little folding stools.

"Well, I knew there was nothing to sit on, and I couldn't see having a good party just perching on the stairs, but if you want to, we can sit on the steps anyway," he said, looking a little embarrassed. "We can use the boxes for tables. Oh, and this giant bottle of water is for drinking if you want it, but it's also for washing your hands afterward. Steve had to turn the water off because of a burst pipe back in September."

"Wow!" Fishel yelled. "This is going to be some fantastic party!" He put Goldie's jar safely on the mantelpiece of the servants' fireplace.

The boys had brought popcorn and soda, all the mothers had baked cakes and cookies, and Fishel's father had donated a bag of all kinds of snacks.

"What a feast!" exclaimed Mr. Sterling.

They all took turns blowing up the balloons and batting them around the room. Mr. Sterling insisted on seeing who could keep a balloon going longest, and though he was pretty good, Fishel won.

After they had all put on the party hats and popped the confetti, they ate. Mr. Sterling seemed to enjoy his first taste of kosher nosh, particularly the Krembos. "And all these homemade things, too!" he said.

When they had eaten all they wanted, they cleared the remains of the food (not much) and the disposables into one of the boxes. After that, they played silly games and sang silly songs that even Mr. Sterling remembered. Then they all put on paper crowns and read out dopey riddles. And Sender turned out to be a real entertainer; he stood up and told one joke after another until everybody was rolling.

Eventually, Mr. Sterling said, "I feel I let you down about using the basement for your clubhouse, you know. But after what happened, I worried that somebody else might break in, somebody even worse than those two thugs. I couldn't risk your safety. When I thought about it that way, I realized the only sensible thing to do was...well, get rid of it."

"But all those memories..." said Sender.

"I took photos of every room before I cleared the house," Mr. Sterling said with a smile. "Maybe I was silly, but at least I can remember it when it was still a home. I wouldn't really want to remember it the way it is now, anyway."

"Did you bring the photos?" Lemel asked hopefully.

Mr. Sterling turned to the old servants' fireplace and took an album off the mantelpiece. "Here you are. I don't think I have to ask you to be careful, but I'm going to say it anyway. Those are my memories."

Making sure the box they chose was sturdy and clean, the boys carefully laid the album down and opened it. As they turned page after page, Mr. Sterling told them which rooms they were looking at, because sometimes it wasn't easy to guess. The pictures showed shabby furnishings and hangings, but it was plain they had been expensive. What a grand home it had been, once!

When they had finished, Fishel said, "That was wonderful, Mr. Sterling! It made the old house come to life!"

"Well, you're going to do that again now." Mr. Sterling grinned, standing up. "I think we should go on a last tour of the house. Everybody has to count the rooms. I've never come out with the same total twice, and neither has Steve. No prizes, but if two people agree, we'll decide that's the right number. I'll write it in on the last page of the album, and all three of you will sign it. Everything counts except hallways, even a little pantry. Turn on all the lights! Be careful for the rotten floors at the top! We'll meet in twenty minutes on the big landing upstairs outside Aunt Louise's bedroom." He held out three sheets of paper and three pens. "Go!"

The boys ran off, laughing wildly, squeaking their party blowers as they went.

Sender ran to the top and worked his way down. Lemel and Fishel worked upward, but Lemel took the servants' staircase and Fishel took the family one. All through the house there were shrieks of laughter and pounding feet.

Mr. Sterling climbed the family staircase when it

was free, up to the big landing. He leaned against the wall and smiled happily. *This house was never meant for only one elderly uncle,* he thought. *It was meant to be full of running children.*

Eventually, Fishel and Lemel came down from upstairs, and in another minute, Sender dashed up the short flight of stairs from the half-landing. He was running so fast, he couldn't stop. He caught his foot in the torn underlay, and crashed headfirst into the paneling!

CHAPTER 17

THE HOLE IN THE WALL

Mr. Sterling was the first to react. He rushed to Sender. "Are you all right?" he asked.

"I'm fine!" Sender said, sitting up, though he was a little dizzy.

Lemel was bending over Sender, but Fishel was staring somewhere else entirely.

"Look! Look!" he screamed. "Look at the paneling!"

Turning to see where he was pointing, they saw that beside the grand marble fireplace, two squares of the paneling had slid aside to reveal a small, dark space. They all crowded around the opening. Within it was a small safe.

"It's a safe!" Fishel yelled. "The missing safe!"

"Do you have the keys, Mr. Sterling?" Lemel whispered hoarsely. "Is the key to the safe on the ring?"

Mr. Sterling's fingers fumbled through the keys. "I-I think so," he said in a shaking voice, holding out a small key. "I think this is the one."

He stepped forward slowly, as if he was afraid to try the key and discover it was wrong. With a trembling hand, he fitted the key into the lock. The boys held their breath as he turned the key. The door of the safe swung outward.

Inside lay a stack of official-looking papers tied up with legal tape. Mr. Sterling's fingers closed around the papers and drew them out. He untied the tape and leafed through a few under the single bulb.

"This is what I've been looking for!" he said softly. "These are the missing shares and investment certificates! My uncle wasn't dreaming after all!"

Sender ran down to the basement and brought up a folding stool.

"I think you should sit down, Mr. Sterling," he said.

"So do I," said Mr. Sterling, sinking down to the low seat. "It's...it's just too much to take in." After a while, he added, "Of course, the investments may have lost their value..."

"They won't have," said Lemel firmly. "They'll be worth all you need. After all this, they have to be!"

"You know, Lemel, I think I believe you!" Mr. Sterling stood up. "I hate to rush you, but to be honest, now that I really have these certificates, I'm desperate to find out what's here and how much I can get for it. Would you mind if we finished up the evening now?"

The boys laughed.

"We were almost done anyway," said Fishel.

"I'll phone you as soon as I hear," said Mr. Sterling.

As they went around the house turning off lights and clearing up in the basement from the party, the boys were a little subdued. Even Fishel, who usually became loudly excited over things, was quiet. Mr. Sterling's wonderful find was simply too important.

It was only when Fishel had collected Goldie and they had gathered outside after Mr. Sterling had locked up that Lemel suddenly said, "Oh!"

"Oh, what?" Sender asked.

"We forgot to use the face paints, Mr. Sterling! I guess we were having too much fun with all the other things you brought."

Mr. Sterling laughed. "We didn't need them, did we? Who has little sisters or brothers?"

"Me," said Sender. "I'm the only one."

"Then take the face paints home for them. They're in the last box we put in the car. And when I've had the house repaired and redecorated, we'll have another party!"

"Are you going to live here?" Sender asked hopefully.

"That's what I'd like to do," said Mr. Sterling, "but I think only on the ground floor. For only one person, it's pretty big. I'll keep the basement for you three."

"Really, for us? Even if you're living here?" Sender's voice was hushed. It was too good to be true.

"Yes, I mean it. I owe you all so much, it's only right to let you share."

"What will you do with the upstairs?" Fishel asked.

"I've been thinking about that," Mr. Sterling said slowly. "That school next door wanted to buy the house, but they couldn't pay what it was worth. Now, what if I rented them all the upstairs rooms — after I fix them up, of course, and make sure the floors are safe — while I lived downstairs? I could break through to their side on the half-landing, and partition off the steps down to my part. Do you think they'd be happy with an arrangement like that?"

The boys considered it.

Lemel said, "They'd probably jump at it, but I know how noisy girls can be. I have a lot of sisters. My mother says none of them run as heavily as I do, but when they scream, it goes right through your head!"

Mr. Sterling laughed. "I like it, all of it — the running and the screaming! It'll be quiet at night, anyway."

They all said their goodbyes. After they had watched Mr. Sterling's taillights disappear into the distance, Sender hit himself on the forehead.

"Oh no!"

"What's wrong?" Fishel asked.

"We forgot to write down how many rooms we counted!"

None of them remembered what number they had come up with. The excitement of finding the safe had driven everything out of their memories. But they still walked home almost in silence, very, very happy.

CHAPTER 18

LEMEL'S CHANCE

The following night was the date for Mr. Berman's speech. After their discovery of the night before, the boys felt it was almost an anticlimax. How could a speaker compare to discovering a hidden treasure?

But the speech was certainly going to be a huge affair. Mrs. Goldstein reported that every single ticket had been sold, and so many people wanted to attend that they'd had to find a bigger hall.

"And you boys are definitely going to be there, don't worry," she told Lemel. "Next to Mr. Berman, you're practically guests of honor."

"Great!" said Lemel.

When he called Fishel to tell him, he immediately held the phone well away from his ear — and just in time, because Fishel's yell of delight practically shook the windows. Sender was just as pleased, though quieter.

"That's a relief. I heard the tickets were selling like crazy," he said, "and I was afraid they'd decide to sell the ones they were holding for us."

After they had lit the Chanukah candles, the whole Goldstein family set out for the hall. As everyone expected, security measures were extreme. Only people with valid prepaid tickets were allowed through the outside door. Ladies had to empty their handbags in front of grim-faced security women, who checked every item; men emptied their pockets and were patted down expertly; every cell phone was confiscated (with a claim ticket given to each owner); wallets, shoes, hats, and beards were examined.

At last, Mrs. Goldstein and Lemel's sisters headed for the women's section, while Mr. Goldstein led Lemel to a seat at the front.

"Wow, you must really have spent on these seats!" Lemel exclaimed.

"Oh, no, mine's at the back," his father said with a smile. "These three seats are for you and Sender and Fishel. Mommy said you'd be guests of honor, didn't she?"

It was pretty lonely there, Lemel thought, until his friends showed up to keep him company. Fortunately, Rabbi Bergman was there too. He was looking a lot healthier than he had a week before, but he looked just as uncomfortable in a front-row seat as the three boys did.

"I don't belong here at all," he told them. "At least you boys did something special. All I did was get kidnapped by mistake!"

"I heard Mr. Berman really feels bad about the whole thing, though," said Sender.

"I can't get over what a nice person he is," Rabbi Bergman said. "He can't stop apologizing — and it wasn't even his fault! He wants to treat Mrs. Bergman and me to a trip to Russia this summer!"

"And he doesn't even know you!" said Fishel.

"Well, he does now, a little. We invited him for Shabbos, and he joined us every evening for menorah lighting. Shabbos in a hotel room all alone is kind of dull. So is Chanukah. We had a lot of fun together."

"Did you play dreidel?" asked Fishel.

"Yes, we did." Rabbi Bergman was grinning.

"Who won?"

"He did, of course!" Rabbi Bergman laughed.

One of the evening's organizers came to the microphone on the stage, tapped it for silence, and welcomed everyone.

"I won't waste your time," he said. "Some of you are here to hear about a *baal teshuvah's* journey. Some of you are here to see a Russian. And a lot of you are here to look at a very rich man. But we've all come to listen to Mr. Mikhail Berman, and here he is!"

Everybody applauded as Mr. Berman took his place at the microphone. He looked tall and athletic, as well as expensively dressed. The spotlights glanced off his gold cufflinks and tie clip. People in side seats could spot his bodyguards in the shadows at the edges of the stage.

So this is what a Russian oligarch is like! Lemel thought.

But when Mr. Berman started to speak, everyone

was so fascinated by his story that they forgot to notice what he looked like. He had been a soccer star himself, on one of Russia's top teams, and still loved the game, but he had discovered that he loved Yiddishkeit more.

"I was earning a lot of money, but I knew it couldn't go on forever," he said, his English slightly Russian-accented. "And I began to think there was more to life than kicking a ball. So I started looking."

Everyone was fascinated by the story of his journey and how he had felt about Yiddishkeit when he discovered it. His relationship with the rabbi who guided him was warm and close, and he had married after becoming *frum*, so his wife shared his new lifestyle.

It was obvious that people would have liked to ask questions afterward, but Mr. Berman explained that he had a busy schedule. But he wasn't too busy to take the boys into a side room for a few minutes after the audience left. They all sat down on some chairs.

"Now we can be a little bit alone," Mr. Berman said.

Fishel looked around at the Russian bodyguards and thought that "alone" meant different things to different people.

"Such an exciting story!" said Mr. Berman. "I want to hear all about it from the beginning."

So, interrupting each other but trying to give him as clear an account as they had given the police, the three boys told him the whole adventure. At the end, Mr. Berman sat shaking his head in admiration.

"I can't get over it," he said. "You boys aren't even bar mitzvah, but you did a man's job."

"We don't want to do anything like that again!" said Fishel. "It was pretty scary."

"And awfully dangerous," put in Sender. "It wasn't just a man's job, it was a police job."

"But you're still three unusual boys," said Mr. Berman. "Your parents and your school must be proud of you."

This is it! Lemel thought. *This is my chance!*

CHAPTER 19

INVESTMENTS

Lemel drew a deep breath. "Mr. Berman," he began, "have you bought that soccer team yet?"

Mr. Berman shook his head. "No, not yet."

"Then I want to suggest a different investment. It gives much better returns than a soccer team, but it takes a lot longer for you to see them." Lemel had chosen his words carefully.

Mr. Berman looked interested but wary. "How would a little boy know anything about investments?" he asked.

"This is a special Jewish one," Lemel said. "It doesn't cost nearly as much as a soccer team. You might even be able to buy the team too, if you wanted to — but you'll be really glad you invested one day."

"Go on. Get to the point."

"It's…it's my school. Torah MiSinai. If you put money into Torah in This World, you see the benefits of your investment in the Next World. And it's a good school. The boys who go there come from families that keep Torah, and the students grow up to be Torah Jews and good members of society. And the school used to manage, until it lost the money from the properties people had donated." Lemel explained about eminent domain and the school's current financial problems.

"That's the cheder you boys go to?" Mr. Berman asked.

Lemel nodded and tried to think of something more to say, but his brain seemed to have shriveled up. "I guess that's all," he finished.

Mr. Berman looked at him for a long time. "Why hasn't anybody else told me about it like that?" he asked. "About investing in Jewish things?"

"Maybe you had to learn to be Jewish first?" Lemel suggested.

Mr. Berman nodded. "It's possible. Look here, Mr. — what's your name?"

"Lemel Goldstein."

"Look, Mr. Goldstein, I'm impressed by a school that turns out boys with the kind of courage and initiative you three kids showed, especially when the police wouldn't listen. Let me think about it, though. No investor jumps into things. What kind of money are we talking about?"

Lemel's heart sank. "A whole lot," he admitted. "Several hundred thousand pounds."

Mr. Berman began to laugh. "That's what people call chicken feed, isn't it? When I'm worth billions?"

Amazed, Lemel stared at him. "But it's such a lot of money," he said. "This affair tonight is to raise money for Torah MiSinai, but it still won't be enough."

"It will be when I'm finished," Mr. Berman said. "Leave it to me. You should go into sales," he added, shaking Lemel's hand. "No, I have a better idea. You three boys are going to be my financial consultants while I'm here!" He looked around at the three of them. "You decide which team I should buy."

Lemel shook his head. "We don't know enough about what you're looking for to advise you."

"Good! You're right!" Mr. Berman grinned. "Can you come to my hotel room for a conference? Maybe right after Shabbos? I can send a car for you. By then my financial adviser will have all the figures and information you'll need to choose for me."

"As long as we can get permission," said Sender, thinking of what his mother had said after he came home from the exciting events of a week before.

However, their parents did give their permission.

And the "car" turned out to be not a taxi but a limousine. Even Fishel was silenced by its magnificence, but it didn't keep the boys from exploring the interior. During the short trip to the hotel, the boys opened and twisted every flap and knob they saw. They discovered everything from an ashtray to a minibar.

"Wow," said Lemel softly. "Wow."

Mr. Berman welcomed them into his hotel room,

which was actually a whole penthouse suite.

"Would you like to look around or see the view?" he asked.

"I think we'd first prefer to get down to business," said Lemel, after a glance at his friends. The other two nodded.

"All right." Mr. Berman gestured, and a man who had been standing by the window came over. "This is Vladimir. He's my accountant and financial adviser. He gives me the figures, but I make the final decision." He laughed suddenly. "He doesn't always agree!"

Vladimir sat the boys down on a long sofa and laid some papers on a coffee table in front of them, explaining that these were the figures for each team and other important information about each one.

For a few minutes, the boys leafed through the papers.

Then Mr. Berman asked, "Well, boys, which is it to be, Whinbury United or Whinbury City?"

"They're both good teams," said Sender. "We know you're just being nice to us — about consulting, I mean — but we discussed the whole idea among ourselves before we came, and we think maybe you really do need our advice."

"We considered all the factors that might affect your decision," said Lemel, "and some other ideas that you might not know about. Fishel did some really good thinking."

Mr. Berman sat forward. "This sounds interesting," he said. "Which team did you decide on?"

Lemel pushed his glasses up and took a breath. "Neither one," he said. "We think you ought to consider buying Millgate City."

"Millgate City!" Mr. Berman leaned back in his deep armchair with a hearty laugh. "They're practically a little neighborhood team!"

"They have big plans," said Sender. "They've just refurbished and expanded their playing field and stands. They want to go places."

"It's like this," Lemel said. "If you buy one of the big teams, they're already at the top. It will cost you a fortune, and they may not even stay at the top. They get, um, complacent, you know, too satisfied with themselves."

"That can be true," Mr. Berman agreed.

"Now, if you buy a team with ambitions, and bring in some really good players — not the biggest stars, but the best team players, who won't look down on Millgate City — they could become as big as either Whinbury team. Like Avis. You know, they try harder."

"It would take time," said Fishel, "and it's a gamble. But that's how you make money, isn't it?"

"Yes, it is." Mr. Berman looked thoughtful.

"There are other considerations, if you go with that choice," Lemel went on. "Millgate's playing field is way over at our end of Millgate, nowhere near the fans. And it causes problems for the *frum* community, especially when they have games on Shabbos."

"It's not just traffic," Sender put in, "it's the type of fans they draw. It isn't really good having people like that walking through a Jewish area just when Yidden are walking home from shul, or their kids are going out to visit friends."

"How would my buying Millgate help?"

"There are plenty of sites available for redevelopment closer to the middle of Millgate, where the fans come from. You could buy a big site there!" said Fishel.

"You can rent out the facilities there for other events, like concerts," Sender added. "And rent out the clubhouse for weddings and things like that."

Lemel nodded. "And then you build housing on the old site." His face lit up. "And think how much you'd make from all that construction!"

"And that isn't a long shot," said Fishel. "It's a guaranteed investment."

CHAPTER 20

NO MORE ADVENTURES!

Mr. Berman looked from one boy to the next. After a while, he shook his head and said, "I was right the first time. You should *all* go into sales!"

Vladimir was relaxing in a chair, laughing quietly. Mr. Berman twisted around in his chair to look at him.

"All right, then," he said. "If you think it's so funny, you can get me the figures."

Vladimir grinned and sat up, saying something in Russian.

"He says he'll have them by tomorrow," said Mr. Berman. "He will. He's a quick worker. Then we'll see if there's anything in your suggestion. Oh — by the way, I've given your school a check to cover the school's debts. The money they raised last week will go toward other things for the school. I'm hoping I have time for a tour of your school too. I bet I can get some ideas for the school my kids go to back home."

Fishel and Sender looked excited, but Lemel's expression was cautious. He had read about the high standards Jewish schools had in Russia. What would Mr. Berman think of Torah MiSinai?

As it turned out, Mr. Berman had so few days left of his British visit that the tour never took place, but he did take a couple of minutes to call Lemel and tell him he was taking his advice. He was going to buy the Millgate City soccer team and do almost exactly as the boys had suggested.

"Vladimir thinks you three have a future as financial consultants," he said over the phone, laughing. "When you finish school, he even says he'll train you!"

Lemel was grateful it was only a joke. He and Sender and Fishel might very well go to work one day, but they had years of Torah study ahead of them first. Lemel laughed back but didn't reply to Mr. Berman.

All he said was, "Everybody's going to be really grateful to you over the new housing, Mr. Berman. I think they should call it Berman Heights, or something like that!"

❧

Life settled back to normal very quickly.

Of course, the fathers of the three boys were all very proud of their sons, and told them so, but they also made it clear that they were still boys and still had cheder to attend and plenty to learn, and that what they had done had been incredibly dangerous.

"If you ever get involved in anything like that again," said Sender's mother sternly, "I won't let you out of the house without an escort until you're eighteen!"

Fishel's parents were even more severe. "You know perfectly well how much you mean to us," said his father. "If you don't have the sense to think of your own safety, think of how we'd feel!"

"You'd break our hearts!" said Fishel's mother, blowing her nose.

Fishel felt so guilty, he didn't even think about going anywhere but cheder for two weeks straight.

"Life isn't always that exciting," Mr. Goldstein told Lemel. "You have to get back to ordinary work."

"I know, Tatty, but we still have the basement of that big house to get together in, and we don't have to think of ways to raise money to save the cheder any longer," Lemel protested. "We can just have fun."

Mr. Goldstein gave him a smile and a pat on the shoulder. "I only wanted you to come down to earth. You have some good work to look back on — as long as you don't get involved with kidnappers again!"

Lemel shuddered. "That was really horrible. I don't even have to promise!"

Eventually, everybody quietly agreed to let bygones be bygones and look only at the good that had come out of the whole adventure.

Work was already beginning on extending the girls' school into the upstairs rooms at the mansion, and Mr. Sterling often invited the boys around to see how beautifully he was renovating his own part of the building.

"I'm restoring it, not just fixing it," he told them. "I've found a very professional firm to do the plasterwork. They usually do stately homes. When they saw what I wanted — that I was only doing a few rooms — they laughed at the little job, but they're doing it anyway. I've even tracked down some chandeliers like the ones I had to sell. Now tell me, what kind of flooring would you like for the basement?"

When he came back, Rabbi Bergman explained to the whole class in detail what had happened to him, and how well it had worked out in the end for Torah MiSinai. All the boys cheered.

"So you see for yourselves how good can come from evil," he said. "I've told you stories about it before, but now you can see it in your own lives. It wasn't pleasant, but, *baruch Hashem*, I had kosher food, I was rescued after only a few days, I didn't miss a Shabbos, I was home in time for Chanukah, and I even had my tallis and tefillin and siddur with me. It could have been a lot worse.

"And now," Rabbi Bergman continued, handing out test papers, "it's time to see how much you learned with Rabbi Markovski while I was away."

Fishel groaned.

ACKNOWLEDGMENTS

This book wouldn't have existed if not for my husband, who thought it was a good idea and encouraged me to write it. I also have to thank my family, who gave me multiple plots, all of which I rejected. I can't remember who suggested the goldfish for a pet, but whoever it was (especially if it was me), you're a genius!

Esther Heller managed the whole project with immense patience; Cindy Scarr was my very sympathetic editor. Both of them allowed me to retain some hints of Britishness in the story. And Avi Katz, who did the cover illustration, drew the house just as it needed to be — the house was based on a real one I had actually been inside (and I never did figure out how many rooms there were).

ABOUT THE AUTHOR

Mrs. Meyer grew up in a small town in the United States, but moved to Manchester, England, years ago. Although she was reading everything she got her hands on, and telling and writing stories from the time she was quite young, she never realized that she wanted to be an author until she already had a large family. She's a great-grandmother now, but she still remembers so clearly how much her own children loved adventure and mystery stories that she thought she'd try writing one for others.

THE MYSTERY OF THE RICH UNCLE

Moish Braverman has better things to do than spend his precious time shopping for his bar mitzvah suit, and one of them is trying to figure out what's going on with his Uncle Feivel Berish. Why has his uncle shown up at the Bravermans' doorstep wearing fancy new clothes, carrying wads of money in his suitcase, and taking endless mysterious phone calls?

As more clues turn up and the suspense rises, Moish fears that his uncle might be in real danger...

STOP, THIEF!

When Sender Edelman moves to sleepy Mersey just months before his bar mitzvah, he knows his life is about to change drastically. But even he doesn't realize what awaits him.

Why are hostile gang members harassing Sender? Will a resentful board member jeopardize his father's job as shul rabbi? Then the shul is vandalized and a precious item stolen. Who committed the crime? Sender is determined to discover the thief and return the stolen item.

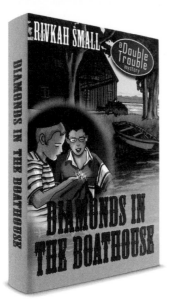

DIAMONDS IN THE BOATHOUSE

On the first day of camp, diamonds are discovered deep in a rotting rowboat.

Who hid them?

Why did they hide them?

And why is an intruder sneaking into the boathouse at night?

In this action-packed mystery of suspense and danger, join two best friends as they set out to unravel the mystery of the diamonds — and uncover a whole slew of sinister secrets about their beloved camp along the way.

A FORTUNATE FIND

It all started at a family celebration at the Kosher Wonton. Meir and his best friend, Shloimy, are excited to see Mr. Cook, their former camp chef, who now works in the restaurant. Their joy quickly turns to puzzlement when Meir's sister Shira notices something strange about the messages in the fortune cookies.

Who could possibly be tampering with the restaurant's fortune cookies, and why? Can Meir and Shloimy get to the bottom of this mystery without ending up in trouble?

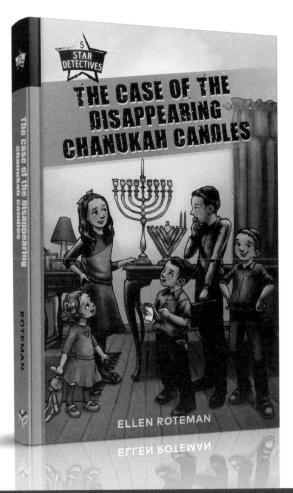